JESSICA WATKINS PRESENTS

TILT MY
CROWN
To The Streets

JOHNAZIA GRAY & DANIELLE OFFETT

CHAPTER ONE

CHAZAE

When I woke up this morning, a nigga knew it was going to be some shit. I just felt it in my gut. Whenever my phone rang off the hook with calls from my workers, I knew that something was going wrong. Whatever the fuck it was, I know I didn't have time for it. It was the first of the month and all I was worried about was collecting my money, distributing these bricks, and going on about my business.

Most of everybody that dealt with me always expressed that I lived my life like a coon. That was cool with me though. I handled my business in the streets and took my black ass right back home to my game system and some weed. My father taught me well and whatever that nigga taught me, that's what I abided by.

Thanks to my father, Dom, the king of New Orleans, I'm considered the mini king of these streets. But see, me, I'm a simple nigga who just wants the money out of this shit. I've never cared for the name brand cars, big time jewelry, video-vixen bitches, and all that other dumb shit these young niggas were into. I'm on a mission and when my father first put me up on game, I knew what I was in it for.

Besides my little brother, Semaj, and my best friend, Tauris, I didn't fuck with these niggas. My workers were strictly my workers. I didn't even make those niggas feel comfortable enough to think we were cool. Well, we were for the sake of my business, but outside of business we were nothing. My trust was slim to none, basically.

The only nigga that I ever looked up to was my Pops. No matter what went down in life, I could always depend on that nigga and I was grateful for that shit. Dom was once married to my snake ass mama, Charae. That was before she turned to the crack pipe and sold us the fuck out.

I remember the days when Charae was the best mother a nigga could ever dream about having. I was crazier about her ass than I was about my pops when I was a little nigga, but I guess shit changed. People change.

When I was ten years old, she decided to get on crack just to grab my father's attention. The shit was crazy because that was the weakest thing I had ever seen before in my life. I do remember my pops being in the streets a lot around the time when she got on drugs, but I also remember him treating her like a fucking queen. He worshipped the ground she walked on and she didn't want for shit, so for her to use my father being in the streets as an excuse, broke my heart into a million pieces. Dom wouldn't admit it, but he loved the fuck out of Charae. When she turned to those drugs, it broke his heart and I could tell, but that didn't stop him from being in the streets. It actually made him go a little harder. I didn't blame him for continuously doing him because that was all he knew, and my mama knew that shit before she even got involved with him.

She always said that by him having Semaj on her was another deal breaker for their marriage, but she never expressed that until she got on drugs. My father slipped up and got Semaj's mother pregnant when I was four. After Semaj's first birthday, his mother was killed when she and her boyfriend's house was robbed. When my father got full custody of Semaj, my mother cared for him, but I could always tell that she only did it out of the love and respect she had for Dom.

Getting on crack and leaving me behind wasn't all she did to shit on us. What put the icing on the cake was when she got herself cleaned up, got on track in life, went and got her degree, then became a fucking attorney. It was one thing to be in a field like that and help niggas out, but she was basically just like rest of these pigs. She was taking niggas like me and my father off the fucking streets and that in itself was embarrassing. Seven years clean and she was one of the biggest and hottest attorneys in New Orleans, Louisiana. When she got clean and found out that I was in the game with my father, she roped me off and made it perfectly clear that she wanted nothing to do with me as long as I was dealing, which was cool. I didn't owe her shit. She left me, it wasn't the other way around. Even still my pops loved her ass like never before; he probably loved the bitch even more now than he did back then. But me and him were two different people in this shit. My heart was cold and she was one of the reasons it was.

After getting out of my bed and checking my trap phone, I checked a few texts and was happy to see the updates. It was some shit going on at one of the traps while I was finally catching up on sleep. Thankfully my right-hand man, Tauris, had got the shit under control before I even got up. I hit him up and he answered on the third ring.

"What's good, my nigga?" he said into the phone.

"What them niggas done fucked up now?" I asked him.

"Money was coming up short, but that was just a misunderstanding. You know once I showed up and showed out, them niggas came to their senses and coughed up that bread. But yeah, that situation is handled. What time you gone be this way?"

I looked at my watch and saw that it was nine in the morning. Damn, I slept long as fuck. "Give me an hour or two. A nigga fade looking a little rough and I got to go chop it up with my pops 'bout some shit."

"That's a bet, bro. I'll be in the same spot until you get here."

"Say less."

I hung up the phone and walked to the bathroom where I handled my morning hygiene. After freshening up, I went into my closet and pulled out something simple and relaxing. The black T-shirt, with a pair of dark blue True Religion jeans went perfect with my fresh black and blue Foamposite shoes. After brushing my hair down and putting my grill in, I grabbed both of my cellphones and I was ready to start my day.

The breeze that New Orleans had to offer had a nigga feeling good as fuck. Wasn't shit like a good breath of fresh air and I was loving it.

I got into my silver Q60 Infiniti coupe that my pops had purchased me for a birthday gift just to shut that nigga up. The tinted windows helped to keep me low-key. For years, I was riding around in a 2000 Honda Coupe which I loved with all my heart. That was my first car and it was definitely my pride and joy. No matter how much work I had to put into it, that mother fucker was going with me to the grave. My pops and brother on the other hand wanted me to boss up a little bit. Shit, with all the money I had I could get whatever kind of car I wanted and some, but I didn't care about materialistic shit. I brought this car out on certain days and I guess it was just one of them days.

When I pulled up to Mr. Chills First Class Cuts, I wanted to turn around. The shit was jammed packed but I knew Mr. Lewis could squeeze a nigga in. When I walked into the barber shop, all eyes were on me. The women who were in the shop drooled at my appearance without any shame. They didn't really care about me though. They just knew I was a young good looking nigga with a whole lot of money. A few of them purposely walked by and brushed up against me, but I wasn't fazed at all. I wasn't a rude ass nigga. I gave them all head nods and kept it moving.

"What's up, man? You came to get that shit cut?" Mr. Lewis and I slapped hands.

"Yeah, squeeze a nigga in. I can't be here all day."

"I'll take you after this little bad ass boy right here." He pointed at the kid who was being pinned down in the chair.

"Hey, Chazae." A familiar voice spoke from behind.

"What's up, Tondra?"

"Ain't shit. Pay for my baby haircut."

I laughed and shook my head. Tondra was a chick I fucked from time to time until we got caught one night by her husband, which turned out to be the pastor at Charae's church. As much as I missed that good ass pussy she had between her legs, I wouldn't dare fuck with her no more.

"You know that pastor got you set. Why you in my pockets?" I licked my lips at her thick, shiny thighs that curved in her short dress.

"Just wanted to see what your young ass was going to say. You know I'm good for a damn haircut." She rolled her eyes.

"You want some of this young nigga dick though don't you?" I smirked.

I handed Mr. Lewis a twenty for her son's haircut.

"Matter fact, just put all his haircuts on my tab from now on," I told Mr. Lewis.

"You ain't shit," he mumbled before laughing.

Johnazia Gray & Danielle Offett

I sat in the chair and waited to get my shit cut so I could be out. My stomach was touching my back and I hoped like hell my daddy was grilling how he normally did on Fridays.

After getting my hair cut, a nigga was feeling brand new. My long beard was trimmed to perfection and it made a nigga stand out. I didn't look to be twenty-three at all but I guess my pops had some good ass genes because he didn't look to be forty-six either. According to the world, I was that nigga's twin.

When I got to my pop's crib, I was happy to see his ass outside drinking a beer and flipping shit on the grill. A nigga was hungry as fuck and a good meal could definitely do me some justice.

"Pops!" I walked up to him and dapped him up.

"I called your ass this morning to let you know that we had a business meeting tonight at seven." He took a swig from his beer before reaching in the cooler and passing me one.

"Should've just texted that shit, man," I told him.

"You know I ain't into all that texting and shit. Just answer the phone and you will be all right. The meeting's at seven pm down at the Pent House club. I got another connect from down south. Little Haitian cat. I wanna see what this nigga talking about with his work."

I let his words process in my head before giving him a nod. "You cutting off our other connect or will we just be adding this nigga on the team?"

"Adding him on the team. It'll be good for business. If he's really up to the part, we'll have more work and money coming in so that means more shit for you to keep an eye on. Did you check on your traps?"

"I'ma go after I finish eating and shit. Tauris got it all under control."

Johnazia Gray & *Danielle Offett*

"All right. Food will be done in about thirty minutes. I got a gift for you in there on the kitchen island too. Let me know what you think."

I nodded my head and walked into the house.

I wasn't surprised to catch Semaj and his little girlfriend, Derria, hugged up on the couch watching scary movies. I don't know what she had done to that little nigga, but his nose was wide open. She had him doing all kind of corny shit just to keep her happy. Like watching scary movies in the broad daylight. That was some corny ass shit.

"Ahhh!" Semaj screamed at the TV.

I fell over laughing. "Nigga, you a bitch. Stop acting like that shit really had you scared." I laughed and took a seat across from them on the sectional sofa.

"Bruh, you got to see this shit. It's real live scary, man."

I waved him off.

"What's up, Derria?" I asked her.

"Hey, Chazae. You chilling with us today?"

"Nah, mama. I got a lot of grown man shit to do today. How did your finals go? I know you was stressing 'bout them shits last time you was here."

"She passed all her classes with straight A's, my nigga. Hit the dean's list and all."

"And you didn't?" I chuckled.

He gave me a slight head nod and looked away in shame. Like he was scared of my reaction. I supported him to the fullest and he knew that. Just because I lived this street shit didn't mean he had to. I wanted better for him. Me and Pops worked our asses off so that he didn't have to. So there was no need to be ashamed.

"No need to be ashamed, man. You're a school boy. You supposed to be making good grades like that. Don't be trying to impress me and act like your ass ain't into them books. That shit is a good look, bro. Keep it up."

"Thank you. I always tell him that shit too, but I guess hearing it from me just isn't good enough." Derria rolled her eyes at Semaj.

"Shut up, girl," he said while playfully smacking her in the face. "But check this shit out, bro. I know you ain't into dating and shit, man, but Derria's best friend is a bad ass bitch and I want to set you up on a date with her." Semaj smiled.

"Don't be calling my friend no bitch, nigga." Derria punched him in his arm.

"My bad, bae, but for real, bruh. This bitch bad as fuck," Semaj said making me laugh.

"You're so disrespectful, Semaj." Derria shook her head and faked offense.

"My bad, baby. You know how my mouth is. I don't mean that shit. Well, most of it I do but you know what I mean." He kissed Derria and she lightened up.

"I'm not into no blind dates. I'ma grown ass man and don't need my little brother trying to pimp me out. I'm just not into dating right now." I shrugged.

Semaj knew I was a street nigga and being a dog was definitely all I knew, so he always insisted to hook me up with bitches with hopes I would run across the right one. I used to date them, but after realizing the hoes was nothing but easy fucks, that made it easier for me to continue dogging.

I hadn't been in love since I was in the eleventh grade and I never tried falling in love again. My first love, Niecy, ruined it for everybody. She was a simple, yet a beautiful chick from the hood. She wasn't one of those girls who dressed in the finer gear and kept her hair done in new styles twenty-four seven, but that's what pulled me into her. That long, thick pretty ass ponytail and those deep dimples was enough to make any nigga at St. Augustine high school go crazy.

She was bad in her own way and I loved her for that shit. When I cuffed her, I introduced her to shit she wasn't used to and because she was grateful, I always treated her ass like the queen she was to me. That was until I got busted with drugs and had to go to a nine-month program. That bitch dropped me like a hot ass potato and got pregnant from a nigga I kicked it with on a daily basis. Shit broke my heart and ever since then, I vowed to never love or trust a bitch. If we wasn't fucking then it wasn't nothing.

"Hook the shit up, man. But your best friend ain't a hoe is she? 'Cause I don't give hoes the time or day outside of their bedroom, Derria."

"She's a good girl." Derria smiled.

"All right, now. I'ma hold you to that shit." I winked at her and walked out of the room.

When I walked into the kitchen and grabbed my boxed gift that my pops had for me, I smiled. It was a diamond Rolex similar to the one he had. That bitch was nice so I took my simple black watch off and replaced it with the Rolex. That nigga was always buying me shit and I never wore it, so to shut his ass down I wore the bitch with pride and happiness. I wouldn't call myself a daddy's boy or nothing because that shit sound gay, but that nigga always looked out for the kid.

Once my pops walked into the kitchen with the finished food, a nigga dug in. I was going in on the meal like it was the last supper. After filling myself up with the ribs, chicken, and sausages, I just needed a fat ass blunt and a bottle of water.

"I got to get going, man, but I'll meet you at the club at six-thirty tonight." I took my pops in for a hug.

"Dress casual and wear that watch. You hear me? That's a nice look for a young boss."

"I hear you, man. See you later."

"Aight, son."

CHAPTER TWO

DOLA

As soon as I opened my eyes, all I saw was a big ass face inches away from mine.

"Good morning, sister girl!" Derria, also known as Ri Ri yelled, a little too chipper for me. She knew damn well I wasn't a morning person but still decided to pop up at my apartment every day like she lived here. For someone who was a full time student, she sure as hell found a way to bother me every five seconds. If she wasn't my baby and I didn't love her, I would take my damn key back.

"Bitch, if you don't back up out my face, I swear I'm gonna slap you." I warned. She laughed, clearly taking me as a joke and jumped on my bed. "Uh uh! If you don't take them shoes off my bed, I know something!" She kicked off her all black Jordan Horizons and got comfortable. It was clear she wasn't going anywhere anytime soon so I decided to get out the bed and take care of my hygiene.

Getting out the bed, I was naked as the day I was born. I always slept this way and as my sister, she knew that so it didn't faze her. I wasn't ashamed of my body so I didn't cover up. Once in the bathroom, I looked in the mirror and admired my beauty. I didn't like to consider myself light-skinned so I'll just say that I'm light brown, standing at five foot four and weighing in at one hundred and fifty pounds. I wasn't fat, but thick I was. I rubbed my manicured nails down my toned stomach before turning to look at my ass. The shit wasn't Nicki Minaj big but it was sitting up pretty like my girl Rihanna. I made it clap one time before brushing my teeth and hopping in the shower.

The water felt so good, I thought I would have an orgasm. Shit, it's been about two years since I had sex so the pressure of the water hitting my cat was the closest thing to an orgasm besides my vibrator. People assumed just because I was a stripper, I was a massive freak but I was the total opposite. Yes, I stripped but it wasn't because I enjoyed it. At twenty-four years old, I did what I had to do to survive. I stripped to make a living for me and Derria. I know what some people think, why not get a regular nine to five? Why not go to school?

My life wasn't my life. My life belonged to Derria and my daughter, Princess. We didn't grow up to crackheads or anything like that. Derria didn't remember our parents but I did. They'd been married doctors who had been deeply in love. They'd loved us and showered us with anything our hearts desired, especially me since I was the oldest. My life was great until I turned eight. On my eighth birthday, my parents were called in to perform emergency surgery. They never made it; a drunk driver crashed into them and their car ran into a pole.

Once the news got out, no one came for us. All the so-called family and friends they had only emptied our home of all of our belongings and were never heard from again. After that, we went from foster home to foster home. I hated each of them. None of them really cared about us. We had the bare minimum of everything–food, clothes, attention, everything. I had Princess when I was seventeen and they let her stay with us, but once I turned eighteen, they kicked our asses out.

The day I left, I knew I had to make some power moves. I started stripping. The first night working at Diamond Dancers, I made enough money to put a down payment on a beat up two

Johnazia Gray & Danielle Offett

thousand nine Honda. After that, I saved up for a two bedroom apartment in the center of the hood. The foster Derria was at during the time didn't give a damn about her, so she was able to move in with me. She stayed with me for two years before she graduated high school and had been attending college ever since. People can say what they wanted, but this stripper money will allow my sister to live her dreams as an anesthesiologist.

I wiped my tears just in time because I heard Derria entering the bathroom without knocking. "Sissy, I can't stay long. I just came to tell you I got all A's on my finals."

I couldn't help the smile that came over my face. I jumped out the shower and ran up to hug her. "I knew you could do it! That's what I'm talking about, Ri Ri!" I yelled. Tears were rolling down my cheeks. I was so proud of her. At times she wanted to give up, but she always kept pushing.

"You're getting me wet!" she yelled with laughter, pushing me away. "Besides, I got a lot more schooling to go. I'm thinking about getting a job or a loan though." She must've seen the look on my face because she tried to explain. "Sis, I'm twenty-one years old. I can't have you going out your way to pay for my schooling. I know how much you hate stripping. I'm tired of you living for me. It's time you live for yourself."

"Nope, not happening. I don't give a damn if you were thirty-one. You're not working until you have that white coat on. Loans are out of the question. Just continue to make them A's and I'll handle the rest." She opened her mouth to plead her case, but I cut her off. "I don't want to hear it, Ri Ri. I told you I got us and I meant it."

Although we were only three years apart, she was my baby. I would die for her, kill for her, anything for that one. She didn't need to stress. That's what I was here for. There was a lot of money in the world and I would do whatever I had to do to make sure she got what she needed.

Ri Ri rolled her eyes and put her hands up in defeat, "Okay, I won't work. Since I made all A's, I just want one thing." The smile on her face let me know it would be some bullshit.

"What is it? Don't ask me about stripping again because you know I will beat yo' ass," I told her with a straight face. Don't get me wrong, my little sister was a beauty just like me. She had that honey brown skin that always looked radiant, those deep dimples that she got from our mom, and her body was all that. She was the spitting image of me. Except while I kept my natural hair curled up and all over the place, she had a perm and let her hair go down her back. She was cute but would never be a stripper. She didn't have the balls anyway. She was green and would be turned out with a quickness.

She bent over and started shaking her ass, making it bounce. I slapped it, telling her to quit. "You know I was just kidding. You know my boyfriend, Semaj's birthday is in a few weeks. He's turning twenty-one and I want to throw him something at the club. I know you don't like me and the girls watching you work, so it can be on a day you're not working."

I had only met Semaj a handful of times but from what I saw, he was a good dude. Although he looked like the common hood nigga, he was in school busting his ass. A few times he had to check Ri Ri's hot ass and make her stay focused. They had study dates and shit. It was the nerdiest yet cutest shit I ever saw. I fucked with him for keeping my sister right.

I nodded my head. "Yeah, I'll hook up a section for y'all. Don't be acting a fool. You know how you get when you drink," I scolded, remembering the last time we went out together and I had to beat some hoe's ass for stepping to her. Yeah, she spilled

Johnazia Gray & *Danielle Offett*

the drink on the girl with her drunk ass but still, that was my sister. Wrong or right, I was coming for that ass.

She gave me a hug. "That's why you're the best. I'm about to go see Ashlee's crazy ass. What do you have planned for today?" she asked.

"You mean Ashlee's thotting ass," I corrected. "But nothing, as soon as you let me finish my shower, I'm going to head out to pick up Princess from Ms. Shirley house and take her to get ice cream or something." I was so tired I didn't feel like going up the elevator to get Princess. Ms. Shirley always kept her when I worked. She was an older lady that was something like the grandmother I always wanted. We met when I first moved into the building and she had been looking out ever since.

"All right. Kiss Lady P for me. Love y'all," she said before leaving.

Once she was gone, I quickly got back in the shower. The water was now freezing cold so I washed up as quickly as possible and hopped right back out. It was a lounge day for me so I wore a blue and white Nike hoodie and grey leggings. I put on my slides and grabbed my purse and keys before heading out the door. Ms. Shirley's apartment was two floors up so I was there in no time. I had a key so I just walked in.

"Mommy!" Princess squealed, jumping off the couch and attacking my legs.

I picked her up and gave her a big hug like I didn't just see her yesterday. "Hey, Lady P. Did you miss me?" I asked her.

She nodded her head and smiled from ear to ear. "Oh my! Is that a tooth missing?" I asked her.

"Yup! It fell out last night. Mama Shirley put it in tissue with salt and put it under my pillow. Guess what happened when I was sleep!" she asked, wide eyed.

Johnazia Gray & Danielle Offett

"What happened?" I asked, faking interest.

She cupped her hands around my ear. "The tooth fairy took it and left me money."

I looked at her as to say "really?" She nodded, clearly blown away by the magic.

"Wow!" I said. "You're really a bigger girl now. Since you're such a bigger girl, Mommy is going to take you to get ice cream."

She jumped out of my arms and started dancing around the living room.

"Chile, if you don't sit ya tail down somewhere I'ma get the switch," Ms. Shirley called out as she entered from the back room.

"Hey, Ms. Shirley," I greeted, kissing her on the check.

"Hey, baby. This little girl right here was about to get popped making all that noise." She looked over at Princess who made a pouty face. She knew Ms. Shirley didn't play and would tap those legs real quick. I didn't mind because she loved her like her own.

"She already ate and bathed so enjoy the rest of the day. You need me to watch her tonight?" she asked.

"Nah, I'm off tonight. Thank you, though. I'll bring you some money when I get back."

Ms. Shirley rolled her eyes and pushed me and Princess toward the door. "Chile, you know your money is no good here. Just make sure you bring me back a scratch off and a pack of Newport's."

I shook my head. "I'm not bringing you back no cigs. They're bad for you, Ma."

"And that shit you called dancing ain't good for you either, but you don't see me talking. Now you better bring my

Johnazia Gray & *Danielle Offett*

cigs back. I'll pop yo' legs too, heffa," she snapped. "Love y'all and be safe."

We walked out and headed to the elevator. "Mommy, why do Mama Shirley got such a potty mouth?" Princess asked. "She always trying to pop somebody."

I couldn't help but laugh. "That's just Mama Shirley for you. She's grown so she can have a potty mouth and you better not disrespect her. You understand?"

She nodded. "Yes, ma'am. She never whoops me for real anyway. I love her. All I have to do is make this face." She made a sad face and poked her lip out. "And then she'll say sorry and give me candy."

I laughed. This girl was too much. She was so cute and could get away with murder.

Walking out of the building, the sun was shining bright and seemed to be beaming down directly on us. I put my hand up to block the sun.

"Mommy, who is that man by our car? He is really tall," Princess said.

I squinted my eyes to get a look at the man she was referring to. *How did he find me?* I grabbed Princess' hand tightly and turned her around. "Come on. We're going to go back inside for a second."

"But why, Mommy?" she whined. "I want ice cream."

"Don't question me. Just come on," I snapped, yanking her forward.

"Dola, don't leave me outchea!" the guy yelled.

This couldn't be happening. I had not seen or talked to Lance in over six years. We left off on such bad terms, I didn't know why he thought it would be okay for him to just pop up in my life and turn it upside down.

"Let me see my daughter!" he yelled.

I stopped in my tracks and turned around. "Nah, Play Boy, this one here ain't your daughter. If it was, she would know you and you wouldn't have dipped out on us like some bitch. Stay away from us."

CHAPTER THREE

CHAZAE

"Odney, this is my son and business partner, Zae. Zae, this is the cat that is supposed to help us become rich men," Dom announced as I entered the meeting room in the back of the club. Both of them stood as I approached. I gave my Pops a hug and then extended my hand to this Odney dude.

"Nice to finally meet you but I think it's the other way around, Dom. You guys will be the ones who make me a wealthy man. I'm trying to be rich like you too," he said. We all shared a laugh as the bottle girl gave each us a shot of Hennessy. Once she was out of the room, we got straight down to business.

"So, wow us, Mr. O," I said, breaking the ice. "Not to be boastful, but we have many suppliers. Like you said, we'll be the ones making you a richer man. We requested this meeting so you must know that we're the ones to get shit done. So…wow us.

Dom looked at me like a proud father on his son's first day of school, but I didn't return the gesture. Instead, I continued to stare at the large Haitian sitting across from him.

"What I tell you, Odney? I told you I was the nice one. My son doesn't play when it comes to the business and neither do I. So like he said, wow us. Why should we work with you?"

My eyes didn't leave Odney. He looked over at me and nervously looked away. What was that all about? What was he hiding? *Strike one*. If he couldn't look a man in his eyes during business, that was a sign disrespect.

Johnazia Gray & *Danielle Offett*

"Well, you guys know that my drugs are out of this world. Anything you want, I have. T's also add a reasonable price compared to–"

I put my hand up to silence him. "We already know you got some good shit. We know your prices are good. We're not asking about your work. Don't try to sell the work. The work is already bought. We want to know about the famous Odney. Why should we choose *you* to work with us?"

He loosened the tie from around his neck. "I am the man for a reason. I've been serving without a hitch which shows that I am off the radar. I say what I mean and mean what I say."

"What about loyalty? Are you loyal?" I asked him.

He shrugged his shoulders. "Yes. As long as you are loyal to me, I am loyal to you." That was strike two. He shrugged his shoulders saying he wasn't sure but his mouth said yes. Which one was it? For him to be *that nigga*, he was unsure of himself.

"I assure you. I have everything you need. When you come on board with my team, you can cut off your other suppliers and we can make each other lots of money."

I looked at him like he was crazy. "Cut off the others?"

He nodded. I looked over at Dom who looked at me but didn't say a word. I had to laugh at this fool. We didn't even shake on anything and he was already requesting cut offs.

"Look at it this way. Once you cut them off, you'll have direct access to me. We can keep the money flowing just between us. I'm pretty sure my price is cheaper than–"

I put my hand up, signaling him to silence. I had heard enough. "Thank you for your time, Odney. We'll be in touch."

He looked over at Dom, but he was already up and ready to walk him to the door. I watched them as they exited. A few minutes later, Dom returned and took a seat. He didn't say

Johnazia Gray & *Danielle Offett*

anything. He just stared at me. He didn't have to say shit because I already knew what he wanted to know.

"Three strikes," I said nonchalantly. Then I downed the shot.

He shook his head. "Here you go with this three strikes shit. This isn't jail, son. You can't just X people out like that. You didn't even give the man ten minutes before you chopped his fucking neck off."

"Pops, you're the one who taught me the game and now you're questioning it? Something is off about that nigga and I'm not going for it. I see pussy in his eyes and the only pussy I fuck with is on a bitch. You know that."

He nodded while rubbing his goatee. "You're right, but trust me on this shit, son. All that shit he was selling, I wasn't buying. We're not cutting anybody off. I just want to use him for a bit and then get rid of him. I don't trust him either so I'll definitely be keeping my eye on him. If this nigga crosses us, I'll personally put a bullet in him."

We dapped up and sealed the deal.

"Damn, why wasn't I invited to the family gathering?" I turned around to see Tauris walking in the door.

"Fuck you. What are you doing here? Ain't no bitches running around," I told him, giving him dap.

"Shit. I thought you said we had a meeting with the Haitian cat," he said. "I just saw that nigga leave."

"Nah, I said me and Pops had a meeting," I corrected. "But I'll fill you in when we get everything together."

He looked pissed. "So, that's how y'all doing it? I thought I was yo' right hand? I'm not allowed in meetings no more?"

Johnazia Gray & Danielle Offett

Pops looked at me before walking out the door. He never cared for Tauris but tolerated him because he knew that was my nigga since the sand box.

"Nigga, get out yo' feelings. You know certain meetings is Pop's shit. I just be tagging along," I told him, downplaying my role in the game. "Once we get shit put into play, you know you gone be the first to know."

He still eyes me like he had a problem. "Yeah, well it sounds like I'm the only muthafucka that don't know shit around here."

"Come on, dog. You know it ain't like that. Don't I put you up on game? Don't even try to play me on no flaw shit. We're brothers first, business partners second," I told him.

He nodded his head and a slight smile came across his face. "You right, bro. I'm just tripping off some other shit. I shouldn't have come at you like that."

I waved him off. "Everything is solid round here."

"Sho nuff. I'm 'bout to head out though," he said. I was leaving too so we both walked to the parking lot. Security tried to follow us, but we declined like we did most nights. We were our own backup. Niggas knew not to try it. If they didn't, they would find out the hard way with three slugs to the chest.

Once inside the car, my phone went off. It was Semaj. "Wassup?" I answered through the car Bluetooth.

"Yo', I know it's last minute but that thick bitch..." I heard Derria cursing him out in the background. "...Like I was saying, the very curvaceous woman wants to do the date tonight. If you don't go, Ri Ri ain't gone give me no pussy tonight." Again, I heard Derria slapping the shit out of him. "You not gone keep putting yo' hands on me, Ike!" he joked, making her even madder.

"I gotcho damn Ike!" she yelled. I heard them wrestling and started to hang up on they love bird asses.

I thought about what I had planned and came up empty handed. I could go home to an empty house like I did every other night, but I was tired of being cooped up in the house. My main line up of hoes wasn't going to cut it tonight. I still wasn't thinking about a relationship but maybe I could get some new pussy out the deal.

"Aye, y'all are killing me with all that fucking noise. I'll go, just give me an hour to go home and change. Text me the spot we're meeting up at."

Finally the wrestling stopped and Ri Ri got on the phone. "Thanks, bro. Ashlee is a real nice woman. She has a lot going for herself." She was really trying to sell her friend to me.

"Yeah, I hear ya, sis. Send me over the info and I'ma meet y'all there."

I hung up the phone and headed home. I'd been doing nothing but working day and night. I didn't even realize that it had been damn near two months since I had some pussy. That was not like me at all. Yeah, I needed some ASAP!

***

I pulled up to Ruth's Chris Steakhouse and saw Semaj and Derria walking up to the door already. Her friend Ashlee wasn't there yet. I stepped out the car and wiped the imaginary wrinkles out of my plain black American Vintage t-shirt and black True Legend jeans. I topped it off with a pair of Zanotti high top sneakers with the golden zipper on the side. It went well with the gold Rolex my pops got me. I wasn't a flashy nigga, but the watch was growing on me.

Johnazia Gray & Danielle Offett

I made my way over to them once I noticed they were waiting for me at the door. I leaned down and gave Derria a hug. "Wassup, Ri Ri." I dapped up Semaj as well.

"Wassup, nigga. Yo' ass holding us up outchea trying to check yo' reflection and shit. Pretty boy ass nigga," Semaj cracked.

I put my fist up in a fighting stance. "Aight, nigga. Don't make me have to chin check yo'' shit outchea."

He waved me off and opened the door.

Once we were seated, the waiter took our drink orders and said she would come back once we were ready to order. We chopped it up and talked about bullshit until I noticed a female walking into the restaurant. My eyes zoomed in on her and watched her every move. She was sexy as fuck wearing a sleeveless, red, half-shirt showing off her slim stomach and tiny waist, matching red pants that all the females were wearing to look thick that were wide at the bottom like some seventies shit, and a pair of black heels. She had the body of a video vixen. Her light-skinned face was perfectly made up—a little too much makeup for my liking but she was cute. Her ass was what made me keep looking because that shit was on Nicki.

"You like what you see?" Derria asked. I took my eyes off all that ass and directed my eyes to Derria. She had a knowing grin on her face.

"I told you the bitch was bad," Semaj added.

I looked back over and the female that I now knew was Ashlee was standing directly in front of us. Derria jumped up to give her a hug. They embraced and did the normal ratchet girl link up.

"Bitchhhhhh! I'm glad you made it," Derria greeted.

Johnazia Gray & *Danielle Offett*

"I know, honey. Sorry I'm late. Trice ass took forever to dye my hair. I said red and she gave me burnt orange." She whined, running her finger through her long extensions.

I took it as my cue to stand up and introduce myself. "Well, nice to meet you, Ashlee, I'm Chazae," I said, giving her a side hug so that my erection wouldn't poke a hole in her ass. She slid in the booth and I sat back down.

I looked at her again and she caught me. She smiled and moved closer to me. "You don't have to sit way over there. I don't bite," she said, discreetly rubbing her hand across my lap and getting a quick feel of my wood. This girl was already trying to freak me and I hadn't even said two sentences to her. I gave her a wink and went back to looking at the menu.

"Damn, Ri. You didn't tell me this nigga was so muthafuckin' fine. I'ma have to trap his fine ass." My eyes shot to Semaj and he choked on his water. "It was a joke," she said, innocently. Innocent or not, I didn't play those types of games. A few women tried to trap me and I personally took them to get a DNA test nine months later. I know a nigga got that magic stick, but damn. Have a baby by a nigga who wants you. See, Zae love the kids but Zae don't love these hoes. My first child is going to be by the woman I choose.

Maybe she was just joking. I didn't want to ruin the date so I changed the subject. "So, Ashlee, tell me about yourself."

"Well, you know me and Derria been friends forever. I love her like a sister. I'm twenty-two. I'm in school for Fashion and Design. I'm a freelance writer for a fashion magazine. I don't have any kids but I want some soon." She gave me a look and I looked at Derria.

Derria chuckled. "Bitch, you so crazy. You don't even like kids."

Johnazia Gray & *Danielle Offett*

"For his fine ass, I will," she said, laughing.

Right on time, the waitress came back and took our orders. I was the last to go. "Let me get the Porterhouse for two, and a side of the lobster." We all passed her our menus and the waitress walked off.

"Damn, I should've gotten the lobster. That sounds so good," Ashlee said, almost moaning.

"You can change your order. She hasn't put it in yet," Derria suggested.

"No, I'll just taste some of bae's," she said, smiling at me. I looked at Semaj who was into his phone. I didn't like the nickname shit especially with a female I didn't know. She was pushing all the wrong buttons and her beauty and ass hypnosis was starting to wear off.

"Not happening. If you want something, order it, my treat." I really wanted to tell her ass she better not touch my food or her hand would come up missing. I didn't play about my food.

My phone vibrated in my pocket. I looked at it to see a text from Semaj.

Bro: I only met the broad twice and she didn't say much. She's bad as fuck but weird. Give her some sperm in a cup real quick. Lol.

I felt someone staring at me and I automatically looked to my left. This chick was leaning over trying to get a look at my phone. Good thing I had the privacy screen protector because she was all in my shit.

"Who you texting?" she asked, almost breaking her neck to look at my phone.

See, she clearly had no idea who I was. I could be a gentleman or I could be an asshole. I didn't give a fuck about a bitch's feelings. I hadn't known her young ass for nothing but a few hours and she was already trying to marry a nigga and have babies. This bitch was crazy.

"Damn, you all up in a nigga phone. Just chill, li'l baby. If you wanna look at something, you can look at this dick," I told her, putting my phone on the table.

She looked at me with embarrassment. It was a shame I had to talk to her fine ass like that but that was the only language some females listened to. That was exactly why these bitches got nothing but deep strokes from me. After that, they were dismissed. All that clingy aggravating shit she was doing was for the birds.

She surprised the hell out of me when she asked to see it.

"Ashlee!" Derria yelled, embarrassed by her best friend's bluntness. I already knew what type of female she was.

"I was just joking, damn. Don't take everything so literal, Ri," Ashlee said, rolling her eyes.

I looked at Ri Ri and she was pissed. "Zae, you didn't have to talk to her like that. She didn't mean anything by none of that. She's just an outspoken person. You're being an ass," she snapped. "And Ashlee, act like you got some class, please."

I shrugged my shoulders. "I only offered to bless her with the dick."

Derria rolled her eyes and began to whisper something to Semaj. Whatever it was caused him to laugh. I checked my phone again and was disappointed to not see any messages or phone calls to get me out of this date from hell.

The waitress returned with our food. I said a prayer and dug in before she could pass out all the plates. I caught Ashlee eyeing my food but I shot her a glance letting her know I was serious. I didn't play about my food. I hate a female who thought it was okay to eat off her man's plate. No, order what the fuck you want and that's what you'll be eating.

"Can you bring me two cups of ice please? I heard y'all have some good ice," Ashlee asked. The waitress nodded her head and walked away.

"Did you just order ice?" I asked her.

She nodded her head. "Mmmmhmm. I love ice. Especially crushed ice. It is so good," she moaned.

I looked at Semaj who laughed, reading my mind. A few days ago, he had showed me an Instagram post about females who eat ice being crazy. I didn't know how much of it was true, but this was the icing on the cake. I already thought the chick was kind of off but now I knew it for sure.

I wiped my mouth with a napkin and threw it on the table. Right on time, my phone vibrated. I didn't even know who it was hitting me up. I took that as an act of God to get me out of this date. I looked at the screen of my phone for a few seconds before jumping up and throwing two hundred dollar bills on the table.

"Some shit just came up. It was nice seeing that ass, I meant you, Ashlee. I gotta go."

I heard Derria and Ashlee calling my name but I didn't even respond. I didn't have time for no crazy bitches. The ice was the last straw.

Once out the door, I pressed the alarm button to my coupe and jumped in. Before I could drive off, I heard a light tap on the passenger window. "See, I knew this bitch was crazy," I said before rolling the window down.

"Look, I'm sorry if I scared you off in there. I'm a nice chick once you get to know me. If I see something I want I go for it," Ashlee said, leaning into the window with bedroom eyes. I knew exactly what it was that she wanted. Even though I knew she was crazy and knew for sure the dick would drive her to jump off a bridge, I couldn't help myself. My man's hanging below was on brick hard and needed some wetness.

"Hop in," I told her.

"What?" she asked, confused.

"You know what you want and I know what you want. So, I'ma give it to you. Get in." I wasn't about to beat around the bush. She wanted the dick and I had the dick. She jumped in the car without another thought. I pulled off and drove a block away.

"Where we going?" she asked. "You live this close?"

I laughed. "You're asking too many questions." I pulled into an empty parking lot and cut the engine.

"Are you kidding me?" she asked.

"Nope." I whipped my dick out and begin to stroke it. "Do you want this dick or nah?"

She looked down and her eyes widened. I knew I was working with a monster. It was ten inches and thicker than a snicker, literally. I measured it once. She leaned over and replaced my hand with hers. After stroking it a few times, she wrapped her lips around it. My head automatically fell back. She began to work her jaw muscles going up and down my pipe. Her mouth was so warm and tight, I felt like I was deep in some pussy.

"Damn, girl" I grunted. With my right hand, I grabbed a handful of her hair and pushed her head down so that my dick could slide down her throat. To my surprise, she didn't gag. "Oh, you don't have a gag reflex either? I like that shit." I began to fuck the shit out of her mouth. The tightening of her jaws and the sounds of her slurping was all I needed to hear. After a few minutes, I yanked her head to the side and allowed my dick to rest on her face as it shot my kids all over her cheek. She tried to move but I held her there until the last drop was gone.

"What the fuck did you do for?" she whined. "I would've swallowed it."

I reached in the glove department and gave her some napkins to wipe the liquid that was now running down her face and to her neck. She wasn't worthy of this nut. Her crazy ass would've probably held it in her mouth until she left and tried to use it. Nope, she wasn't about to turkey baster trap me. Females were crazy enough.

"My bad," I said, nonchalantly. My phone vibrated and it was Semaj.

"Yo'," I answered.

"Aye, Ashlee's crazy ass went running out after you and she ain't been back. You saw her?" he asked.

I looked over at Ashlee who was still wiping her face. "Yeah, she right here. We were getting some shit straight. She's coming back in now."

He said all right and hung up.

I started the car and headed back to the restaurant. "Wait, you're not going to give me any dick?" she asked.

I looked at her and back at the road. "Nah, maybe next time."

She mumbled something under her breath but I didn't understand her nor did I want to. Once we were back at the spot, I pulled up front to let her out. She didn't get out right away. She sat there just staring out the window.

"Well maybe we can finish up later. I can give you my number," she offered.

I shook my head. "Nah. I appreciate the head but I'm straight. I'll see you around though." She looked like she wanted to cry but instead she jumped out the car and slammed the door.

Johnazia Gray & Danielle Offett

I waited until she made it inside safely before pulling off. I couldn't even lie, Ashlee had some bomb ass head. I loved a female that didn't gag, but all I could think about was how crazy she already was. If the head was good I just knew her pussy was even better. Then, I would've fucked her again because it was good and she would start going even crazier on a nigga. I couldn't afford them problems. It was sad that the crazy ones had the best pussy. That was why I had to leave her crazy ass right where I found her.

CHAPTER FOUR

SEMAJ

I cruised the streets with my brother and my nigga, Tauris as we headed to the car dealership so I could get my baby a new car. I didn't know what it was about Derria but she definitely had a nigga's heart. When I was with that girl, I was genuinely happy and she brought a side out of a nigga that I couldn't explain. She was down to earth, smart, and beautiful.

The day I met her on campus, I knew that she was going to be mine. A young nigga felt comfortable with Derria. I could be myself, you know? Having money didn't move her one bit. She just loved me for me and that wasn't usual due to me coming from money. When I hooked up with bitches all they saw were dollar signs, but it wasn't like that with Derria. She hated when I brought her gifts weekly. She thought because I was used to gold digging bitches that that was the reason I was spoiling her so much, but it wasn't. I just wanted her to be in the finer shit because she deserved it. My baby was focused on school and getting multiple degrees and I was definitely going to be the nigga to push her, especially since I knew how important having an education was.

I lit the blunt of loud that was sitting in my ashtray and took a long pull out of it. After a few more puffs, I passed it to my brother.

"Better not be no bap ass weed, my nigga," Chazae said right before hitting the blunt and choking on it.

I laughed. "My shit is never bap. Copped that shit from a white cat on campus. I think he grow the shit in his pops garden."

"Damn, man…let me get that nigga number so I can set some shit up with him. This shit is straight gas." He passed the blunt to Tauris.

I wasn't sure what was on Tauris' mind but for the entire day, that nigga had been quiet. We all grew up together and I knew when something was wrong.

"Tauris you good back there, my man?" I asked him.

"I'm good. Why you ask?"

"Just checking. Your ass been quiet. I'm here if you need to talk bro."

"I'm good little nigga," He puffed on the blunt. "This shit is burning though. Definitely need to put this cat on the team."

"If I can trust him." Chazae shrugged.

Tauris sucked his teeth and waved Chazae off. The nigga was definitely in his feelings about something.

When we pulled up to Toyota of New Orleans, I had already spotted the car that I wanted to purchase for my baby. The red 2016 Toyota Camry would fit her perfectly. Not to mention that red was her favorite color. All it was missing was a big ass bow tie on it.

The boys and I got out of the car and took a walk around.

"This little hoe got your nose wide open, bruh. Is the pussy that good?" Tauris frowned.

"First off, bruh, don't call my lady a hoe. I don't disrespect Shunta's hoe ass and she deserves to be called all the names in the fucking book. Secondly, my nose may be a little open for her. She a good ass girl who ain't fucking the crew like *Shunta*. All she do is go to school and pass her classes. She deserve this shit, my nigga. Chill out."

Johnazia Gray & Danielle Offett

Tauris was always shading a nigga when it came to females but he had no right whatsoever. His old lady Shunta had fucked the entire Magnolia projects and nobody passed judgment against him for loving that bitch. I wasn't ashamed to say I was in love. Hell, after all the fucked up relationships I had been in, I was glad I finally came across a good girl that I could spoil and not have to worry about feeling stupid over in the end.

"You different from us, nigga. If you want to treat your girl, treat your girl. Derria's a good chick. You hear me?" Chazae placed his hands on my shoulders.

That's why I loved my brother, man. No matter how that nigga felt about women not being shit he never tried to force me to feel that way. My big brother was a very positive influence and I loved him for that shit.

"I got a question, bruh, and I don't want you to flip out on me." I looked at my brother.

"Run it, nigga. Don't beat around the bush." Chazae looked me dead in the eyes.

"I know you don't want me into this shit, but I've been watching you and pops and I'm ready to be in with y'all. I'm tired of y'all taking care of me. Let me work for it, bruh."

"Nigga, are you dumb or are you dumb as fuck?" Chazae snapped.

"Man, chill out with all that. You got to feel where I'm coming from."

"I ain't got to feel shit. This shit ain't for you and you know that, Semaj. What the fuck you want to get into this shit for? It ain't shit but stress and headache. Every day me and pops out here in these streets, we don't know if we coming home in peace or if we'll even make it to see the next day. This ain't your life, nigga. Just focus on school. If you want to work for money go get you a nine to five. You'll still have income from me and Dom, but getting in on this shit ain't even up for discussion." He stormed off.

For the longest I had been going to my brother trying to get him to put me on, but he wasn't having that shit. Even though I was pissed the fuck off that he was still treating me like a young nigga who didn't know shit, I understood where he was coming from. My brother just wanted what was best for me.

"Check this out, bruh. I got some business I'm doing under the table for myself. You can run for me, Chazae ain't even got to know," Tauris whispered.

"What kind of business you talking, my nigga?"

"Some work I copped for myself to sell. Chazae know I'm doing my own thing. He don't mind, but I'd love to have you as one of my runners. You my brother and I can trust you like that. The shit will be so fucking easy and your pops nor Chazae will know that you're involved in this shit."

I smiled bright. That's why I fucked with Tauris. He stayed looking out.

"Sounds promising." We slapped hands.

"First meeting tonight. I'll text you the address and shit later."

I nodded my head and walked into the car dealership to cop my baby her gift for passing the semester. I couldn't wait to see the smile on her face.

***

"Okay, can I take this shit off now?" Derria sat on the sectional in my father's living room with a blindfold over her eyes.

"Dom in here while you doing all that cursing." I laughed.

Even though we had a cool ass father, Derria hated to curse in front of him. She would always go on about how her sister didn't raise her like that and shit.

"I'm so sorry, Mr. Dom," she apologized.

"Can we just get this over with, Semaj? She's had the thing over her eyes for about ten minutes now." Ashlee rolled her eyes.

That was exactly why I didn't want that hating ass bitch to help me. She was just jealous of my baby. All I asked her was to bring Derria over. I didn't ask her to stick around.

"Derria, I just asked you to bring her over here. If you're impatient just leave, ma," I told her.

"Straight up," Chazae cosigned.

She flicked a bird at him and he laughed. She was still salty that my brother wouldn't give her any dick.

I grabbed Derria's hand and led her outside. I had her car parked perfectly on the lawn.

"You ready, baby?" I stood behind her and whispered in her ear.

"Yes, baby. I am," she said sweetly. Damn, her voice made my dick jump but that could come later. Right now was all about her.

I took the blind fold off of her eyes and her mouth dropped.

"Semaj, a new car?" she said just above a whisper. Her teary eyes was confirmation that she was appreciative of what I'd done for her.

"Thank you so much, baby," she cried and hugged me.

Johnazia Gray & Danielle Offett

"Why you crying, baby girl? You deserve this. You worked so hard for it and I know you didn't want to stress your sister for a new one." I kissed her and handed her the keys.

"Come take a look at it with me, Ash." Derria waved Ashlee over.

"Okay." She smiled. Her smile didn't reach her eyes so I knew it wasn't genuine.

When she opened the door to the car and saw all of the dozens of roses that were wrapped in the front and backseat, she cried and wiped her tears.

"This is so sweet, baby. Thank you so much." She cried and hugged my neck tight.

"Guess what else?"

"What?" she smiled.

"Two weeks after my birthday we're going to Miami for a week. How that sound?"

"Sounds good as hell to me, baby. But I'm glad you didn't pick your birthday because I have something special planned for you." She pecked my lips.

"Damn, can we have him for his birthday?" Chazae joked.

"Nope." She laughed.

After taking her car for a ride around the block, she and Ashlee came back to the house.

"I'm cooking before I leave tonight if you girls want to stick around," my pops said.

"I think the fuck not, man." Chazae frowned.

"Why are you so shady?" Ashlee asked him, sadly.

"The only person shady around this bitch is you. Your ass wasn't even happy for your friend today. Had your stuck up ass face turned up the whole time. I bet you ain't even record her special moment did you?" Chazae snapped.

"It wasn't like she was getting married or anything." She rolled her neck.

"Keep her from around you, Derria. I know a snake when I see one." Chazae laughed and bit his banana.

"You need to chill, Chazae. That's not nice," Derria said, feeling sorry for her friend.

I wasn't about to check my brother because I felt the exact same way.

"I'm gonna leave. I'll see you later, Derria." Ashlee grabbed her bag.

"Wait up, friend. I'ma go with you."

"Nah, this our time together." I pulled Derria onto my lap.

"It's cool, friend. Spend some time with your bae. I need to go home and get ready for my date tonight anyways." She smirked at Chazae.

"Don't suck his dick." He laughed.

"Aye! Chill out, man," my father told him.

Once Derria and Ashlee was outside, my father almost chewed Chazae's head off.

"If I ain't never taught you shit I taught you to respect ladies. You tripping."

"That hoe hating on little sis, man. I'm telling y'all. She's a little salty slut."

"Watch your mouth. You got to be careful on how you treat that girl. That's her best friend at the end of the day."

"You right. I'll apologize to Derria, but I meant every word. Then you offering her to kick it with us for dinner. That girl sucked my dick an hour after we just met. I don't need nobody like that around me."

"I feel what you saying, but next time, handle it like a grown man." Dom walked upstairs.

Johnazia Gray & *Danielle Offett*

"I'm glad you did her little hoe ass like that, bro. Derria will have to learn for herself though," I told him

"She will." He nodded his head.

"What's up with Tauris, though? That nigga's attitude been a little wild these last couple of days."

"I don't know, but I'ma find out."

As much as I wanted to ask him if he really knew that Tauris had plans to push some work under the table, I wasn't going to do that. Tauris had never sold us out or did no flaw ass shit so I was just going to go along with the flow.

CHAPTER FIVE

DOLA

Ms. Shirley and Princess sat at the round table in the dining room. Ms. Shirley was always so good to me and my baby I decided to return the favor. For weeks she had been complaining about no one ever cooking for her, so that was what my day consisted of. Her favorite food was oxtails and yellow rice so I made sure to put my foot in it. The oxtails fell off the bone and the yellow rice was just how she liked it. She loved cabbage, but me and Princess hated them so I made her a huge pot of them to take back to her apartment. The strawberry cheesecake that I made for her was delicious as well. Ms. Shirley taught me how to cook everything, but due to me always being so busy I never had a chance to cater to her, but that was about to change.

"Chile, you sure did make me happy with this food today," Ms. Shirley said, cleaning one of her oxtail bones.

"Yeah, mama, it's good," Princess said with a mouth full of food.

"Swallow your food before I tear your behind up, gal," Ms. Shirley threatened.

"Sorry, Ma Shirley," Princess apologized after swallowing her food.

"I'm glad you liked it, Ma. I've got to start cooking for you more." I held small conversation as I cleaned the kitchen.

"Did you make sure to leave Derria and Semaj a plate?" Ms. Shirley asked me.

Johnazia Gray & *Danielle Offett*

"Yes, ma'am. I put their plates in the microwave. They should be here any minute now."

"Okay, good, because my babies need hot meals on their stomachs. Derria told me how Semaj's father is always cooking. I'm glad she has someone besides me to depend on for a meal because Lord knows you'll let that girl have fast food every day."

"That's all she likes anyways." I shrugged.

"Tell me something, Dola. When are you going to let that guard down and let a man love you?"

"Ma, not tonight okay." I rinsed the final dishes and placed them on the counter.

"You don't never have time to talk to me, so why not tonight?"

Shirley walked into the kitchen with her and Princess' plates and began washing them in the sink.

"I got it." I took the plates from her.

"You're beautiful. Even though you're working at that club I know it's only to support your sister and this child here. I see men try to talk to you in the building all the time. Why you won't try out dating one of these days?"

"I don't trust men and you know that."

"I know you're young and you better let what your ex did to you go. That was in the past, Dola. This is now."

When I was seven months pregnant with Princess, I was contacted and told by Lance's other baby mother that she was seven months pregnant as well, with twins. Not only did it stress me out completely, but because of all the stress I almost lost my child. Because I was young and dumb, I tried sticking around and playing the rider role, but that just wasn't for me. Numerous nights, Lance wouldn't come home. I couldn't count on my fingers how many times his baby mother and her sisters jumped on me. It was ridiculous and he did nothing to stop it. I loved Lance more than I loved myself and that was when I knew I had to let him go. When we left Chicago and moved down to New Orleans, I hadn't heard from Lance and he never even tried to reach out to my baby. I kept up with him on social media though only to find out that he was living the happily ever after with the same bitch who almost drove my ass crazy.

Fuck niggas. I didn't have time for them and their bullshit.

"I know–"

"Hey, hey, hey!" Derria and Semaj walked through the door and I was glad. Shirley could finally get out of my ear with the love talk.

"Hey, my sweet baby. Come give me some suga." Shirley opened her arms for a big wide hug.

"Hey, Ma Shirley. Look what me and Semaj picked out for you today."

When Derria pulled out the Estate 18 KT yellow gold, diamond, and pearl ring, Ms. Shirley's eyes watered as tears fell down her face.

"This is exactly the same ring my mother left me, Derria." She hugged her tight.

"Aww…Derria and Semaj, that was so nice." I rubbed Ms. Shirley's back.

Ms. Shirley always told us how she could never get over losing her mother's ring in her apartment years ago and Derria went out of her way to make sure she got another one just like it. I was feeling like a proud big sis. That was so big of my little sister for her to even think that deep.

"How much did y'all heifers pay for this?" She wiped her tears.

"A few thousand." Semaj shrugged.

"Okay, big money," I joked.

Everyone laughed.

"I love this gift. Words can't express how grateful I am. Thank y'all so much." She placed the ring on her finger. "Even though this isn't the one my mother left me, I'm going to make myself believe it is. It is the exact same one. It makes me think of my mom. Thank y'all again." She hugged them both.

"Y'all plates are in the microwave" I told them.

"You want to eat here, baby?" Derria asked Semaj.

"Yeah let's kick it here today," he said.

"Where's Lady P?" Derria asked.

"Princess ate her food and went missing in the back. She's probably back there playing with her karaoke machine if she's not sleeping."

"Thanks, Semaj." I smiled at him.

"For what?"

"Making my little sister happy. I love it and I love you for it."

"It's nothing. That's my duty, sis. I love your sister."

"I keep trying to talk her into getting a man, but she's so crushed from a damn relationship from years ago," Ms. Shirley told Semaj.

"You're really going to tell my business, Ma?"

"Everybody know it. As much as that boy has been over here he can tell your ass ain't never had a man over here."

"I got somebody for you. You and that nigga will be perfect." Semaj rubbed his hands together.

"I don't think so." Derria cut her eye at him.

"Why not?" Semaj asked him.

At that point I was lost on what and who they were talking about.

"We'll talk later, but no."

"Man, they'll be perfect, bruh. Let me call my brother."

"No, I don't date, Semaj. Don't worry about what this nosey old lady is talking about right here."

"Who you calling an old lady? I got yo' old lady, heffa!" Ms. Shirley snapped.

I rolled my eyes and turned my attention back to Semaj. "Like I said, I don't date."

"You don't date *yet*." He chuckled, pulled out his phone, and hit a few buttons. "Aye, bruh, I just need one favor. Please my nigga." He put the phone on speaker.

"What's up?" I assumed his brother said.

"Derria's older sister is for you, man. I swear she's the one," Semaj spoke into the phone.

"Nah, man. I'm done with those blind dates. Hell nah. Relationships just ain't for me. Let's leave it at that, man."

"They're not for me either," I agreed.

"Man, all right. You gone die lonely, my nigga."

"And Dola is going to die an old, lonely heffa too," Ms. Shirley agreed.

"That's cool. Hit me later and not about no dates when you do," the guy spoke into the phone.

Semaj hung up and looked at Derria who was eating out of both of their plates.

"And leave it at that." Derria raised her eye at Semaj.

"All right. Give me my plate, nigga."

We all sat around the table and caught up with everything. This was the first time that Semaj had spent almost the whole day with us and I liked him even more. He was such a gentleman and

Johnazia Gray & *Danielle Offett*

his father did an amazing job raising him. Things really took off when we played a game of spades. Semaj and Ma Shirley sure did make one hell of a team because they kicked me and Derria's ass every round.

"I think I need to get going. I have church in the morning. Are you coming with me, Dola?"

"Yes, ma'am. Me and Princess will be there. Let me walk you upstairs." I grabbed her purse and the pot of greens.

"I'll see y'all later. Thanks again for my special gift." Ms. Shirley kissed them and waved goodbye.

When I opened the door, I wanted to slam it when I was face to face with Lance. I was at a loss for words.

"What are you doing here, Lance? You need to leave!" I said on the verge of tears.

"Nah, just let me come in and see my daughter," he said.

I couldn't lie. Lance was looking so fucking good. After all these years, he still had that handsome baby face that I had fallen in love with. His chocolate skin was so smooth and that smile was still beautiful. He smelled good as hell.

"Well are you going to let the child in?" Ms. Shirley asked.

"No, Ma. I don't want him in here."

Derria walked to the door and frowned. "This nigga got to be crazy," she said.

He smirked. "What's up, li'l sis?"

"Never claimed you as my brother, nigga. You need to leave."

"Not before I see Princess." He crossed his arms over his chest.

"Just cut it out and let the young man in, chile."

When Ms. Shirley walked over to the sofa and sat down, I knew it was about to be some shit. As much as I didn't want to let this nigga in my house, my comfort zone, or around my child, it was still his baby—even though he ran out of her life like a little bitch.

"Come in, but you can't stay long." I rolled my eyes and let him in.

When he sat across from Ms. Shirley, I knew she was about to question his ass something serious, but that was cool with me. Anything to make the time go by faster.

I walked back to Princess' room and my baby was sleeping peacefully in her bed, hugged up with her teddy bear.

I gently shook her to wake her.

"Yes, ma'am?" she whispered.

"Get up for a minute, baby. I want you to see someone."

She wiped the sleep from her eyes and grabbed my hand while holding her bear in the other.

When we got in the living room, she spoke to everyone. "Hey, Titi. When'd you get here?"

"A while ago, baby. You were sleeping when I first walked in so I didn't want to bother you, honey bunny."

"Heyyyyyy, that's the guy that was standing by our car the other day, Mama." She pointed at Lance.

Lance stood and took his hat off. When he walked over to Princess, he kneeled down on one knee and looked her into her eyes.

"Hey, Princess. I'm your dad."

I don't know why but for some reason my heart felt like it was breaking in a million pieces. When Princess began to cry, that didn't help the painful feeling at all.

"Why are you crying, mama?" I asked her.

Johnazia Gray & *Danielle Offett*

"Because, Mommy. I've missed so many daddy-daughter dances and you said that my daddy wasn't here. You said you didn't know where he was."

"Tell her the truth, Lance. Let my baby know that I wasn't lying to her." Tears fell from my eyes.

"Your mommy wasn't lying to you, baby. Daddy made some horrible decisions in life and I'm sorry. You didn't deserve to miss any of those dances and I promise you that I'm going to make it up to you." He wiped Princess' tears but mine continued to flow.

The look that he gave her was so genuine and sincere it tugged at my heart. What brought him here out of all places? Did he come to look for us? My mind was all over the place.

"Does that mean I'm going to be spending more time with you now?" Princess asked him.

"Yes, baby. You have two sisters that I want you to meet too." He pulled out his phone and showed her his twins.

I wanted to fall out. For some odd reason, after seven years, I still felt disrespected when he talked about his other two daughters. He had them on me for crying out loud.

"Wow, I have sisters?" Princess asked, excitedly.

"Yes, love." He kissed her cheek.

"Okay, it's time to go," I told him. "Let me walk you outside. Can you please help Ms. Shirley upstairs with her stuff, Semaj?

"Yeah, sis. You good though?"

"Yeah I'm good. No worries."

Lance chuckled. "Yeah little nigga, she good."

"This ain't even what you want, bruh." Semaj lifted his shirt.

"That's enough. Come on." I grabbed Lance's hand.

Johnazia Gray & *Danielle Offett*

When we got outside to his car, I lost it and started to attack him. I punched him over and over in his chest and he stood there and took it.

"Why did you come back?" I screamed and cried. "Huh? Why did you come back? To ruin our lives some more?"

He took me in for a tight hug and I didn't fight it. He held me so tight.

"You left us. You left her, Lance. Why did you wait so long to come back?" I cried.

"I fucked up, Dola. Just let me make it right." His voice cracked.

I shook my head.

"Make it right with Princess," I said before turning to walk away.

He grabbed my hand and pulled me back into his embrace.

"Is it too late for me to make it right with you?" he asked.

"Nigga, it was too late when I first left Chicago." I walked away, leaving him standing there looking crazy as hell.

When I walked back into the house, Semaj and Derria were looking at me with pity eyes.

"I'm okay," I lied.

"No you're not, Dola. You're not okay." Derria hugged me and I cried some more.

When Princess came out of the bathroom and saw me crying, I wanted to get myself together for her but I just couldn't. I couldn't bring myself to it.

"Mommy, why are you crying?" Princess asked, on the verge of tears.

"I'm so sorry, Princess. Don't cry. Mommy's just going through something."

Johnazia Gray & *Danielle Offett*

"Should me and Semaj kick it here with you for a little while longer?" Derria asked.

"It's cool, Ri Ri. I'm about to take a shower and get my baby ready for bed. Thanks for hanging with me." I hugged her and Semaj.

"It's not over, sis. I'll see you in church in the morning."

"Okay, and I got that set up for you." I winked at her.

"Thank you." She smiled.

***

"Oh my God, sis. Everything looks so perfect in here." Derria kissed my cheek.

We were in the club before the doors opened and the decorations for Semaj's surprise party were off the chain. Even though me and some of my friends from the club were the ones to decorate everything, it still looked amazing. I was glad that I could put a smile on my sister's face.

"I'm glad you like everything. The bar is unlimited tonight as well." I winked at her.

"You're the best." She kissed my cheek again.

"I'm always the best when I come through for you." I laughed.

"Whatever. You know I'm always appreciative." She playfully punched my arm.

"I know and that's why I will always give you anything that you want and need." I returned the kiss on her cheek.

"Show time is in an hour, sis. Be on time." She grabbed her keys and her drink from the bar counter top.

"I'll be here. See you later."

"See you."

"Your little sister is bad as fuck," the Latino bartender complimented.

"Thanks, girly, but she's not into hoes." I smirked.

Girly was always hitting on any bad ass female that came into the club. She wanted me to be gay so bad it was crazy.

I headed home to get dressed and ready for the night. It had been a while since I stepped out and actually enjoyed myself. Even though I saw Diamond Dancer's Club every damn week, it felt good to know that I wasn't going just to dance tonight. They had the best drinks and I was looking forward to them. I just hoped and prayed everything turned out right for my sister and her boyfriend. I wanted nothing but the best for them.

Princess was staying the night at Ms. Shirley's house and I was glad. Ever since the day Lance showed up, he had been coming by every day to see her. It was so weird that she fell in love with him so fast and easy. I wasn't knocking it, though. I just needed him to stay the fuck away from me.

After walking into the house and freshening up, I opened my make-up box and decided to beat my face. The look I gave myself was simple yet classy as hell. My highlight was popping and you couldn't tell me shit. I redid my sew-in and the bob was hot. Instead of wearing my bob straight, I curled it into big, loose, bouncy curls. It was last minute but I knew that it would go perfect with my dress.

After slipping the black mesh, prime mermaid see-through dress over my body, I took a look at myself in the mirror and smiled. I looked amazing and the ass that I had was like *wow*. I had to admit that dancing toned me out perfectly. I looked good and I wasn't ashamed to toot my own horn. The dress was so bad and I was glad that I went with it. My breasts sat up so perfectly in it and my curves would definitely make the niggas turn their heads tonight.

I applied some nude lip gloss on my lips, sprayed my body with the *A Thousand Wishes* fragrance from Bath and Body Works, and I was ready to go. As I cut off all the lights in the apartment to leave, I heard a knock at the door. I knew it was Lance because lately he'd been the only nigga who was comfortable popping up at my house. I took a look at myself in the long mirror in the hallway and walked to the door with my heels in my hand.

"Who is it?" I yelled.

"Lance, Dola," he said.

I snatched the door open. "What's up?" I asked him with a straight look on my face.

"Damnnnnnnnnnnnn. You look good as fuck, baby mama." He licked his lips.

"Princess is upstairs at Ms. Shirley's house." I pointed upstairs.

"A nigga just was in the neighborhood working and I needed to pee. Do you mind?" he asked, inviting himself in.

"Actually I do, Lance. You got a dick. You could've peed outside."

"I wanted to pee here." He walked to the bathroom.

"Hurry up and get out," I snapped.

Once he was done using the bathroom, he grabbed me by my hand and pulled me close. When he sniffed my neck and kissed it, my panties flooded with wetness.

"You smell and taste good." He gently nibbled on my ear.

"Stop," I moaned and pushed him. "If you continue to not respect me and my space, I'm going to stop your ass from coming over here all together. I'm not fucking playing."

"Whatever, man. I'm 'bout to see my baby and be out." He walked upstairs.

Once I got into my car and headed to the club, all kinds of shit was running through my mind. I couldn't wait to get me a strong ass drink.

It wasn't even one 'o'clock yet and the damn club was jammed packed. The lines were wrapped around the building and the parking lot was on swole.

I took a final look at myself in the car mirror and put on my black red bottom pumps.

When I walked through the VIP line, all of the men was reaching for my hand, but I paid them no mind. I only came to turn up with my sister for her man's birthday. Once I got into the club and heard the trap music that was bouncing from the speakers, I was ready to turn up. I walked over to the bar and ordered a few shots of Hennessy. After throwing them back, I was ready to shake my ass a little bit.

After spotting my sister and her crew in their VIP section, I walked over to them. Access was granted as the security guards flirted with me like always.

"Just say the word right now and I'll marry your ass," Big Jay whispered in my ear.

"In your dreams, you can have whatever you want." I laughed.

When I walked over to my sister, she stood up and hugged me. She was looking so beautiful in her sheer sequin mini dress and the matching pink Giuseppes were to die for. Her little thot ass friend, Ashlee, on the other hand was looking basic as usual and she didn't look happy one bit, but I guess that's because she was sitting to the side by herself.

"You look so fucking good, sis," Derria slurred.

"You do too, drunk ass," I giggled.

"Let me introduce you to everybody. You already know my baby, Semaj." She pointed. "This is his brother Chazae." She pointed again and I was at a loss for words. I didn't even hear the other people's names she was calling out because my eyes were glued directly to him.

The way he bit his bottom lip and sipped from his cup while staring at me had me going fucking crazy. It had been a minute since I saw a good looking nigga that had me in a trance just from his appearance. I didn't even know the nigga but I wanted to know everything about him.

"Damn, y'all are eyeing each other the fuck down." Derria laughed.

"Girl, is that the one y'all was trying to send me on the date with?" I sat next to her and asked.

She nodded.

When Ashlee went and sat next to Chazae, I already knew what was up, but the good thing about it was that Ashlee wasn't my friend. I didn't give a fuck about her feelings if she wasn't his girl.

"Your girl feeling a little jealous, I think." I laughed and sipped my drink.

"Behave. She likes him but he's not interested." Derria shrugged.

"He a single nigga. Holler at him." Semaj nodded his head toward his brother.

I wouldn't dare approach him first but I definitely had my eyes on him.

When Nicki Minaj's song, *Truffle Butter* came on, I walked to the dance floor and started shaking my ass to the music. I was feeling damn good off my drink and I was determined to

Johnazia Gray & *Danielle Offett*

have a good ass time. After working up a sweat, I walked over to the bar and took a seat.

"I know you don't mind me sitting here," Chazae sat next to me and whispered in my ear.

I smiled and shrugged.

"Whatever she want plus a few shots of Patrón on the side." He told the bartender.

Once I downed my two shots of Hennessy and he downed his shots of Patrón, he got up and walked behind me. "I don't even know what it is about you, mama. But you mine and don't even know it."

He kissed my neck and walked away.

"Give me two more shots!" I yelled at the bartender.

CHAPTER SIX

CHAZAE

"I don't even know what it is about you, mama. But you mine and don't even know it."

I kissed her neck and walked away, cursing myself as I walked back to the section. Like really, Chazae? Did you just say some corny ass shit like that to a female you barely know? I plopped down in a booth next to Semaj. He looked at me with a goofy grin on his face.

"I told you she was the one, bro," he repeated, taking a bottle of black Hennessy to the head.

I waved him off. "Fuck these bitches."

My eyes made their way toward her like they belonged there. She was back on the dance floor dancing with Derria. I watched her every move. She danced like she owned the place. She was dancing so sexy, I wanted to yank her little ass off the dance floor and sit her on my lap. That wasn't even like me.

Once I saw her walking back to our section, I tried to look away but for some reason my eyes landed on hers as soon as she entered. "You mind if I sit here?" she asked, sitting next to me and using my shoulder as a crutch as she removed her heels. "My feet are killing me."

I didn't have a foot fetish but she had some pretty ass feet. I hated females who came to the club wearing those open-toed heels and chipped nail polish. If you can't afford to get your feet done, you can't afford to be in the club.

"Damn, nigga, you wanna suck her toes? Somebody give bro some hot sauce," Semaj joked.

I shot him a bird and looked away. This nigga had really put me on the spot.

"How you gonna say that shit to me at the bar and walk off?" she asked. It was good to know that my words were still on her mind. That meant she was feeling a nigga.

"You'll know why very soon." I gave her a wink.

She shifted in her seat and I could tell I had her wetter than a faucet.

I took a shot of the Hennessy that was on the table. I didn't know if it was the liquor or if it was her, but something was happening to me and I was feeling her ass. *Nah, Zae, you don't do relationships. You don't do one bitch. You do everybody's bitch,* I told myself.

The moment I looked over at her, the little voice in my head began to sound stupid. I admired her beauty. She had on makeup but it wasn't caked up like most of these bitches. It was just enough to bring out her features. Her soft curls made me want to run my fingers through them. My hand went out to touch them but I put it back down. Yeah, I was tripping.

"Dola, I know today's your day off but I need you, baby." I looked up to see the owner, Chance, standing in front of us. We went way back so I knew he was cool.

Dola rolled her eyes. "Really, Chance? My one fucking day off and you need me?"

"Come on, don't do me like that. Trixie was supposed to be the main act for tonight but her son got rushed to the hospital. I got some big people in here tonight. I *need* you."

I was just sitting back, listening to the conversation. Was she a stripper?

Johnazia Gray & Danielle Offett

Dola downed a shot before jumping up. "You owe me, Chance. Sorry, I gotta go," she said to me.

"You work here?" I asked, already knowing the answer.

She nodded her head slightly before walking off with Chance on her heels. Damn, the one female I was somewhat feeling was a damn stripper. I didn't fuck with strippers. I would fuck them but I didn't fuck with them how I'd planned on fucking with Dola. I shook my head. She was just like the rest of these Instagram famous hoes.

"All right, coming to the stage is our top of the line diamond girl. I hope y'all stole y'all mama's rent money because you're gonna need it. Coming out is the one, the only, Blaze!"

As soon as the name left his mouth, a ring of fire shot up from the stage followed by smoke. The flickering lights made it look like a fire drill was going down. All the men ran to the stage to get a better look. Whispers could be heard as they tried to look through the smoke. Once the smoke cleared, the stage was empty. Even I looked around to see where the dancer was.

Rihanna's "Sex With Me" began to blare through the speakers.

"Sex with me, so amazing
All this hard work, no vacation
Stay up off my Instagram, pure temptation
Hit a switch on a fake nigga, like a station
Sex with me, so amazing
Sex with me, so amazing"

Suddenly, Dola, dressed in a fire red teddy came twirling from the ceiling. Once almost at the bottom, she opened her legs straight out and landed in a split. Seductively, she leaned on her back and closed her legs before tumbling over and landing forward. Like a cat, she crawled around the stage. She leaned forward, arched her back, and made her ass clap toward the crowd. All the men went wild.

"Damn," I whispered. Dola was really killing the stage but I still couldn't believe she was a stripper.

"You like what you see, bro?" I heard Semaj yell over the music.

I didn't respond. I couldn't respond. My head was everywhere.

"Happy birthday, Bro." I took another shot and got up. "I'm out."

"What, why?" he asked, looking confused. "Yo' girl is performing."

I looked at the stage and our eyes connected. "Nah, that ain't my girl."

I walked toward the door. Even though she was a long distance away, I could still feel her eyes burning a hole through my back. As bad as I wanted to turn around, I couldn't. There was no way I could take a stripper bitch seriously.

***

"So you gone sit in my whip and not say shit?" Tauris asked, blunt dangling from his lips. "Rude as fuck to not talk to me in my own shit."

"Nigga, stop nagging like you my bitch. Light that shit up and puff- puff pass," I told him. "Over there begging for attention and shit. You wanna check my phone too?"

Using his knee to steer the wheel, he lit the blunt and took a pull before passing it to me. "Fuck you, nigga. Speaking of bitches, I heard you was drooling over some stripper bitch."

For some reason, him calling her a bitch didn't sit too well with me. "Don't call her a bitch, bro. I wasn't drooling over nobody. She was just cool peoples. Nothing more, nothing less."

"Damn, don't tell me you got hit too? First Semaj and now you." He shook his head. "Never thought I would see the day it was hoes over bros."

"You know me so chill out with all that love shit. Where we headed anyway?"

"To the mall. I gotta go get Jr. some shoes. Shunta keeps bugging my ass talking about his shoes too little and shit."

I looked at him like he had lost his mind. "Nigga, you wildin'. That's yo' son and you don't know when he needs new shit?"

He shrugged his shoulders.

"You a paid ass nigga. There is no reason yo' little ones should go without. You should have him shit to last a lifetime. Tighten up, bro."

He smacked his teeth. "What, you my daddy now, nigga? Always trying to run shit. Don't worry about my kids. I got this," he said, turning into the mall.

I dropped the subject. I wasn't about to argue with him over his family. If he wanted to be a no-good ass daddy that was on him. I made a mental note to drop some shit off to Shunta for the kids on the regular since this nigga couldn't do it.

He parked the car in the handicapped zone.

"Nigga, you ain't no damn handicapped. Park somewhere else."

He pulled out a handicapped sign from his glove compartment and put it on his mirror. "I got the hook up at the DMV. I can get you one too. Just say the word."

"Nigga. You handicapped all right. In the fucking head. Take that shit down and go park somewhere else," I barked, jumping out the car. "Doing dumb shit, trying to get locked up for no reason. I'ma catch you inside."

He didn't even let me move away from the car before he sped off. I swear he was having mood swings like a bitch lately.

"Fuck him."

I walked into Oakwood Center Mall and immediately remembered why I didn't come to the mall. It was too packed like a can of sardines in this muthafucka. I hated to be around a lot of people.

I made my way through the mall to the Burberry store. I picked up some more of my signature Burberry Touch cologne and a few more items before heading to Footlocker to see if Tauris had made it in yet. I was sure he did; he was just in his feelings and didn't want to call me.

"I told you to buy my baby some shoes not fuck the shoe bitch!" a lady yelled.

"Man, what the fuck are you talking about? The bitch is helping me pick out shoes!" Tauris yelled. Getting a little closer, I saw that it was his baby mama, Shunta.

"Wassup, Shunta." I said. Tauris dogged her ass but it had nothing to do with me. She was cool people when she wasn't spazzing out on his ass. I respected her for being the mother of his child, something he should've been doing.

"Wassup, Zae. Ask yo' no-good ass friend what is up since he wanna be up in here fucking shoe bitches," she spat, mugging the girl who was clearly just doing her job.

Tauris rubbed his hands over his waves and grunted. "Man, gone with the bullshit. I just told yo' simple-minded ass I ain't fuck her. You said Jr. need some shoes and that's what I'm doing. Damn! Let a nigga nuts breathe."

As they argued, the shoe attendant looked terrified. She looked to be about seventeen and it was probably her first and last job thanks to them. I passed her three, hundred dollar bills and apologized for what was happening. She took it and walked off toward the back.

"Don't try to walk off now, bitch!" Shunta taunted, attempting to go after the girl. She was a straight hood bitch that acted up at any given moment. Tauris grabbed her by the arm and told her to chill.

"If you ain't fuck her then let's do a balls check," she told him, folding her arms.

He looked around to make sure no one heard her. "What? Gone with that crazy shit." He tried to walk off but Shunta was all over him trying to stick her hand down his basketball shorts. I had seen enough. I walked out the store.

My phone went off and it was Pops. "Wassup?"

"Somebody stole the cookies from grandma's house," he said. I could tell he was pissed.

I stopped walking. "The main house or the shed?" I asked, praying that he didn't say the main house.

"The fucking main house. Handle it like yesterday." He hung up.

"Shit!" I cursed. I made an about face and headed back into the store. Tauris and Shunta were wrestling and the manager was threatening to call security.

I walked over and grabbed Tauris. "Fuck all the bullshit. We gotta go. Grandma called," I told him.

"Shit!" he yelled, pushing Shunta off him.

Johnazia Gray & *Danielle Offett*

We damn near raced to the car. Someone had hit one of our most profitable stash houses. Out of all these years, no one was bold enough to do so. This came left field but I was prepared. I needed answers and I was going to get them.

CHAPTER SEVEN
CHAZAE

"I'ma ask you one more time. Who sent you?" I asked, sweating profusely.

Once I'd arrived at the stash house yesterday, the damage had already been done. The money was gone and all but one worker was dead. We took a big loss and I didn't take too kindly to losses. The money could be replaced but my time and the loyalty these men had to me couldn't. It hurt most to know that I would have to send them home to their families in body bags. Somebody took out the niggas I was responsible for and I wanted names.

One good thing was that one of the workers, Londo, was upstairs when everything was going down. After the commotion settled, he shot the remaining few intruders and left one for me to question. I immediately ordered him to be taken to the warehouse until I made it.

Now, it was torture time. I had been beating him with my specially made whip for the past thirty minutes. It wasn't just any whip. It was made of thick chain and had a nail in each one. Each time it made contact, it would pierce the skin. I called it my chain of pleasure. I wasn't a sadist but torturing got my adrenaline rushing.

My victim, who was hanging from a rope by his hands, was bleeding heavily. There was a puddle underneath him. He was going to die soon but before he did, I needed answers. I

Johnazia Gray & *Danielle Offett*

wiped his blood off my hands onto my shirt and pulled his wallet out my back pocket.

"Drayton Kemiris Thompson. Age twenty-six. Address is 3499 South Claiborne Ave. New Orleans, Louisiana." His swollen eyes tried to widen but were still in slits. "Yeah, I know where you live. Londo, give this to Mannie and tell him to get me everything on Drayton Thompson. I need to know where his family stays, where they're buried, I want it all." Londo took the license and walked out the room.

"If you don't tell me what I want to know, Dray, everyone you know will die. Everyone that is dead, I'm going to unbury them and put them on the doorsteps of your loved ones. Do you know how terrifying that would be?"

He nodded.

"I'm not gonna lie to you. You're going to die regardless. Don't you want to save your family?" I asked.

I heard him mumbling. "What he say y'all? Take the tape off his mouth."

My enforcer, Bruce, went over and snatched the tape from his mouth dramatically. He screamed to the top of his lungs. "Nigga, stop being a bitch," Bruce yelled.

"Fuck you!" Drayton spat. I had to give it to him. He lasted longer than a lot of other niggas and he still managed to talk to shit. But just like the rest of them, he would talk.

"Enough of the pissing contest. Let me hear it."

"Look, all I know is that some nigga approached me and my niggas and asked us to run up in one of yo' spots. Said we could keep whatever we took."

"Oh yeah? How did that work out for you?" I asked.

Bruce tapped me on my shoulder and handed me an apple. He knew torturing made me hungry so we had a fridge off to the side. I bit the apple six times and it was gone. "Thanks, man."

I finished chewing before I spoke. I had manners and shit. "What else you got for me, Dray? I hope that ain't it."

"That's all I know," he said.

"Well, that ain't good enough. Damn, I thought I was gonna let your family give you a proper burial. Bruce, handle it."

Bruce walked over from the torture table holding a blow torch. The blue flames shot out. "Time to have some real fun," Bruce said with a wicked grin. I loved the adrenaline but Bruce loved the pain.

Dray began to wiggle and shake. "Okay! I'll tell you. Tell him to get that shit away from me." Bruce had the torch right next to his face. "Augghhhh!" Dray yelled.

"All right, Bruce. Play nice. He got something for us. Talk to me, Dray. This is your final chance.

He took a deep breath and shook his head. I allowed him a moment to get his thoughts together. I already knew what was running through his mind. He never thought he would be the one to snitch on a nigga but here he was.

"There's a group of them. They came from up north to take over. They got a plug or some shit and was told all they gotta do is take you and your crew out," he said.

"What's the nigga in charge name? What does he look like? I need details."

"I don't know what he look like." Bruce lit the torch causing him to scream. "Just chill, man! I—I—I don't know what he looks like. Never even saw that nigga. All I know is that his name is Lance. Every time he rides through the hood, he's in an all-black Charger with tinted windows.

65

Johnazia Gray & Danielle Offett

"Man, you know how many black Chargers is outchea?" Bruce asked.

I rubbed my goatee in thought. "Out of towners, huh? Which means out of town license plates." Even though I expected more information, Dray wasn't who I wanted. He was just the nigga sent on a suicide mission.

"Thanks for your time, Dray," I told him, standing up.

"You gone let me go?" he asked in disbelief.

I laughed. "Of course not, but since I see that you were just grinding for your family, I'll pay for your funeral. Do ya thang, Bruce."

I heard him screaming and I heard the sound of Bruce lighting his ass up. Once I exited the warehouse, it was silent. From the outside, no one would never know of the events taking place just a few feet away.

I hopped in my car and headed to Pops' crib. We had a lot of unanswered questions but a lot more information than we had yesterday.

"Call Tauris!" I yelled to the car.

"Calling Tauris," the car responded.

"Wassup," he answered.

"Nigga, don't wassup me, Why the fuck you didn't meet up at the spot like I told you?" I barked. He dropped me off at my car and he was supposed to meet me at the warehouse. The nigga never showed up.

"My bad, some other shit came up with one of my bitches. Where you at? I'm gone pull down on ya."

I gripped the steering wheel. Instead of handling business, he was worrying about some bitch. "Nigga, we just got hit and you worried about a bitch? Fuck them bitches. Meet me at Dom's now!"

Johnazia Gray & *Danielle Offett*

***

"What the fuck is wrong with you, Zae? If you wanted to be in the torture house why did you hire Bruce?" Pops asked, sitting behind his desk. "You're supposed to keep your hands clean now."

"You told me to handle it, and I did. I got some information. So, the li'l nigga told me it's some out of town niggas here trying to take over. I made a few calls and found out the niggas are from Chicago." Now I had his attention. "The head nigga name is Lance and he's driving a black on black charger."

Dom laughed. "You know how many wanna be hood famous niggas ride around in a black Charger? Ha! Good luck with that."

"True shit, but how many niggas got Chicago license plates outchea?" I asked him. "We get niggas from all over, mainly New York and Atlanta but rarely Chicago. It shouldn't be that hard to find them."

"A'ight. Well it seems like you got everything under control so I'ma let you handle it." The doorbell chimed and he went to answer the door. I was right behind him.

"Why you ain't use your key, son?" Dom asked as Semaj, Derria, Ashlee, and Dola walked in behind him. She was looking good as hell in a pair of blue jean shorts and a blue and white striped shirt. She reminded me of Debbie from down the street off the movie Friday.

"Tried to show you some respek. You know you be having naked bitches running around," Semaj joked. Derria punched him in the arm and gave him the evil eye. We had that

Johnazia Gray & *Danielle Offett*

kind of relationship with our pops but she didn't like it. She thought it was disrespectful.

"Bae, hit me again and I'ma tear yo' little ass up," he warned, picking her up. She wrapped her legs around him and screamed frantically. "We'll be out back by the pool," he yelled over his shoulder.

"Don't be fucking in the pool with y'all nasty ass," I yelled.

I looked at Dola and she tried not to look in my direction. The way she looked at everything else including the ceiling let me know she was avoiding eye contact with me. I know she was mad at me. The last time I saw her, we were at the club and I found out she was a stripper. I never fucked with a stripper outside of the bedroom but for some reason, I was still feeling her. No matter how much I tried to block her from my mind, she was still on it.

She took her red, curly hair and tucked it behind her ear. Was she nervous to be around me or was she fighting the urge to slap me? "Do you mind if I use your restroom?" she asked.

Dom pointed to the kitchen and told her it was the door on the left. She walked past me like she didn't even see me. I watched her until she turned the corner. I wanted to go after her, lock her in the bathroom and fuck the shit out of her, but I didn't want to risk the chances of her trying to turn up on my ass. I would definitely get up with her later.

I felt someone staring at me so I looked to my left. Lo and behold, Ashlee's thirsty ass was looking at me like she wanted to jump on the dick. "You wanna show me where a bathroom is at?" she asked, licking those dick suckers she had for lips.

"Nah, follow the yellow brick road and figure it out," I told her before going out back. I found Pops lighting the grill and Semaj was all down Derria's throat on the side of the pool.

"It ain't Friday, Pops. Why you grilling?" I asked him.

"I can't grill for my family?" he asked, flipping the burgers. "I invited you boys here because I have some family business to announce."

"What kinda family business?" I asked him, curiously.

"Don't be looking at me like that. I'ma let y'all know later. Nothing to worry about though, I promise. Just some shit we gotta discuss that's all."

"Is it deep family business, because I invited Tauris over here so that we can discuss this bullshit with those out of town niggas."

Dom gave me a look before taking a swig of his beer. "You know I don't trust him, right?"

I waved him off. "Come on, Pops. You know me and Tauris been kicking it since grade school. That's my brother from another mother."

"He gotta be from another father too because that snake ass nigga ain't come from my ball sac," he spat. I couldn't do anything but laugh.

"Stop doing my dawg like that. I'ma let him know I'ma meet up with him later." I shot him a text letting him know that Pops needed to talk to us about some family shit and that I would get back up with him later.

His text came back in record time.

Tauris: Smh. Family meeting, huh? Guess I ain't family.

I didn't have time to stroke his ego and be with all that soft shit. I would just let him be in his feelings until we linked up later.

Like a magnet, my eyes turned and made their way toward Dola. She walked over and sat next to Derria by the pool. They were laughing and talking about something. I wondered if it was about me.

"You feeling her," Pops said, with a smile.

"Nah, she cool though," I told him nonchalantly.

"Boy, I'm not asking you shit. I'm telling you that your young ass is feeling her. I've known you all your life so don't lie to me, lie to these hoes."

I waved him off and went back inside. Pops was taking too long on the grill and I was hungry as fuck. I decided to munch on my last banana. That should've held me over until he was done. I looked on the counter and it was gone.

What the fuck?" I said out loud. Somebody took my banana. They knew I loved fruit. I barged back outside and up to Semaj. "Nigga, I know you didn't eat my banana."

He looked at me and laughed. "I know yo' ass ain't out here trying to check me over some damn fruit. Fruity ass nigga," he joked.

"I'm sorry, Zae. I gave it to my sister. I didn't know it belonged to you," Derria said, apologetically.

I looked over at Dola, who was eating the banana without a care in the world. As she chewed the banana, my eyes zoomed in on her lips. She had some sexy ass lips. I pictured her wrapping them around my banana.

"Take a picture, it'll last longer," she said, rolling her eyes at me.

"Damn, li'l baby. Why you gotta act like that?" I asked her, taking a seat next to her. I tried to put my arm around her but she moved it.

70

Johnazia Gray & *Danielle Offett*

"Don't come over here acting like we cool. You dipped on me without saying shit. Is it because I'm a stripper?"

Derria and Semaj could tell things were about to get heated so they dismissed themselves.

I could tell she was really bothered by my actions. Honestly, it was because she was a stripper but the more time I had away from her, I thought about how dumb it was. She was a stripper but I knew it was for a reason. Just by looking into her brown eyes, I could see the pain and hurt. She couldn't have been doing it because she liked it. I wanted to know more about her.

"Don't act like that, li'l baby," I said, trying to get closer to her. She was still being stiff toward me. "All right, I'ma keep it real with you. Finding out you was a stripper kind of caught me off guard."

"Chazae, I need to talk to you real quick." Me and Dola looked up at the same time to see Ashlee standing in front of me with her hand on her hips.

"No you don't, ma. Move around," I told her, trying to be nice.

She clearly wasn't having it. "Oh, so that's how you gone try to me play me? So you don't fuck with me no more?" Her voice went up a notch and I wasn't feeling it.

"Ashlee, don't come with this shit. Only thing I fucked was your mouth. Sorry, but that was it. Don't embarrass yourself. Move around."

She opened her mouth to speak but Dola cut her off. "Just because you're Ri Ri's best friend don't mean I won't lay hands on you. I already don't like yo' ass. You see us talking. If he wanted your services, he woulda asked." She turned to look at me. "Babe, do you need your dick sucked?"

"Nah, not unless it's from my woman," I responded.

"Okay, so he declined your services. Bye, Felicia!"

Ashlee rolled her eyes at both of us and stomped inside the house.

"So I'm babe now?" I asked.

Dola rolled her eyes and returned to acting stiff. "Like I said, we ain't cool. I'ma stripper bitch, remember?"

"Come on now. Just listen to what I'm saying. You know how many stripper bitches I run into trying to set a nigga up and run my pockets? All the strippers I know are money hungry bitches only out for a dollar. Strippers got a bad taste in my mouth. I'm not gone lie to ya but you, you're different. I never met a female that made me want to know more about them besides what the pussy feels like."

She looked at me like she wanted to slap the shit out of me. I threw my hands up. "I'm just being honest, li'l baby. That's how I know I fuck with you. I'm sorry for leaving like a li'l bitch. I shoulda let you know straight up. Look at me." I used my finger to turn her face toward me. "I'm sorry, li'l baby, and I wanna start over. Can we do that?"

I looked deep into her eyes as she searched mine for the right answer. I wasn't asking her to marry a nigga or nothing like that. I just wanted a chance to see what was really up with her.

After a long pause, she extended her hand. "My name is Dola. It's nice to meet you."

I took her hand into mine and kissed the back. "My name is Chazae, but you can call me daddy if you're nasty." I blew her a kiss and she burst into laughter. Even her laugh was sexy.

Finally, I got her to smile. "Boy, you are something else."

"Aye, the food is done but I need everybody to meet me in the family room first," Dom yelled. I guess it was time to make his big announcement. I prayed like hell is old ass didn't get nobody pregnant. We followed him into the family room.

"Wassup, Pops?" Semaj asked, pulling Derria in his lap.

He smiled as he looked at everyone. "Where's poollee?" he asked.

"Oh, she wasn't feeling well so she dipped out," Derria replied.

He nodded his head. "Good because this is a family meeting. Derria, Dola, I know it hasn't been long that I've known you two but I consider you to be nothing but family. My sons are lucky to have you." Dola shifted in her seat but gave him a smile. I winked at her causing her to blush.

"Sons, I wanted to let you know before the streets told you. I'm being investigated."

Everything else that came out of his mouth fell on deaf ears. This news just hit me like a ton of bricks. Investigated? He ran a tight ship. Only a select few knew of him and his business. What was really going on?

Semaj was up and pacing back and forth with Derria trying to calm him down. Dola moved closer to me and put her hand on top of mine. That small gesture meant a lot.

"I don't know all the details yet. A friend of my mine works for the Bureau and he gave me the heads up that my name landed on the captain's desk. No warrants or red flags have been issued so I'm in the clear. That's why I need you to keep your hands clean, Zae. Semaj, I heard about you wanting to get in the game. That shit is dead. I need you to keep your head in the books. Until I get shit under control, I need everything kept at a minimum. Understand?"

Semaj nodded his head in understanding but I just stared at him. He could fool Semaj with that everything would be okay shit but I knew better. If the Bureau was sniffing around, it was for a reason. There was a snitch in the camp and I needed to know who. We fed everyone and treated everybody like family. Someone had the balls to rob one of our stashes and give Dom up to the law. Who was it and why?

CHAPTER EIGHT
TAURIS

A nigga had absolutely no intentions on going to that fucking warehouse for the bullshit because I knew exactly who was behind the shit, and I didn't give a fuck to be honest. I was so sick of playing the underdog to these niggas. When my cousin, Lance, came to me and told me he needed to get back on his feet, I guaranteed him that I had something set up for him. So far, the shit was going just how we planned. It was my job to repay my cousin for everything he had done for me when I was a little nigga. Lance's mama, Tanya and my mother were full-blooded sisters. When my mother got strung out on drugs and I was sent to New Orleans to live with my grandma, Tanya always made it her personal business to send for me so that me and my cousins remained close. Lance always took care of me and looked out for me. They never made me feel like outsiders or made me feel beneath them how Chazae did when he came up. I honestly loved Chazae and Semaj but I didn't care for those niggas. They were born with a silver spoon and they didn't understand how I felt when they treated me like I was a sidekick. Chazae always tried to act like I was just as much of a boss as he was, but he and his father's actions said otherwise. I wasn't even allowed at the fucking family meetings, but we were supposed to be brothers.

Semaj was smart when it came to those books but he wasn't street smart, and I knew that I could get some shit done with that nigga on my team. I didn't understand how they wanted that nigga to claim to be a man and they was taking care of him like he was a bitch. He was no better than me and Chazae and he was going to get a taste of these streets. No one was going to get hurt behind this shit, but with Lance hitting Chazae's traps up, I knew for a fact that shit would humble him and he would come off that arrogant ass high horse.

I pulled up to Dom's house and almost rolled my eyes like a bitch when I saw Chazae's car parked on the lawn. I didn't feel like hearing the nigga bitch about that petty ass hit, and from the hot ass text messages he was sending my phone, I knew that shit was bound to get ugly. The first meeting with Lance was scheduled in about two hours and I was only coming here to pick Semaj up so that we could get to the meeting in time.

After smoking my blunt down, I threw my hoodie over my head and knocked on the door. Semaj opened the door and stood there and looked at me with a look of sadness on his face.

"The fuck is wrong with you, nigga?" I asked him.

"Pops is mad as fuck, my nigga. Shit is fucked up." He shook his head, "They're in his office."

"I'll be in there shortly," I told him.

"I'ma take a step outside and smoke this blunt," he said with a lost expression on his face.

I nodded my head and entered Dom's office. He and Chazae were lost in conversation and no one even acknowledged the fact that I was standing there.

"Have a seat." Dom pointed to the chair next to Chazae.

I did as I was told and looked him directly in the eyes. From the look of it, that nigga actually looked like he had been crying. If he wasn't sitting in front of me, I probably would've laughed. All of this behind a hit? That was exactly what the fuck I was talking about. Hits were meant to happen and they were in here sobbing behind it like a bunch of bitches.

Johnazia Gray & *Danielle Offett*

"Why weren't you at the warehouse when your trap was hit, man?" Dom asked me. He had a stern look on his face like he was ready to dig in my ass.

"I'm sorry about that, Dom. Man, Shunta ass is pregnant again and I had to rush her to the hospital due her having complications," I lied.

"So you couldn't pick up the phone and say that, nigga? I was blowing your shit up and you was straight ignoring me. That ain't how shit go, especially when you're in this business," Chazae snapped.

"Man, nigga, I don't give a fuck about business when my baby mama is in pain with my child. She was hurting. Your ass is always bitching. You know if it wasn't important then I would've been there. So chill the fuck out!" I snapped.

"Bitching? Nah, nigga, you've been the only one walking around this bitch acting like a bitch lately. Ain't no bitch in my blood and I don't give a fuck at the end of the day because you're the one responsible for paying the plug back. That's your fucking trap that you were assigned to run. I just don't like how your ass been handling your shit lately. You been moving around in these streets all wrong my nigga."

"Nigga, you got me fucked up. I'm not paying shit."

"Nah, he got it right. That's your trap, right?" Dom interfered.

"That's my trap but since when did we have to pay the plug when our traps got hit? If that was Zae's trap, would he have to pay?"

Dom stood.

"If that was my fucking trap it would've never gotten hit in the first place, nigga. Fuck you mean?" Chazae barked, puffing his chest out.

Johnazia Gray & Danielle Offett

"Are you questioning how I run my shit, Tauris?" Dom asked, calmly.

"I'm not questioning shit, but I'm simply asking if that was Chazae's trap would he have to pay the plug out of his pocket?"

"Hell fucking no he wouldn't have to pay the plug shit if that was his trap because I got him and whatever he makes is his. I'm his father and I'm responsible for him, but I taught the both of you niggas how this shit goes so you should know. But to answer your question, no, absolutely not. He wouldn't have to pay the plug because his father would pay it for him. Your trap got hit, which means it's your loss and you will be paying. Now any more questions?"

"Man, I'm out. Just text me how much I need to pay." I got up.

"Let me know if this is too much for you. I can always get a hungrier nigga who takes this shit serious." He shrugged.

"I got it, man." I stormed out of the house and got into my car almost forgetting that Semaj was supposed to be riding with me to the meeting.

When he got into the car, he shook his head. "How come you missed the meeting, nigga?"

"Semaj, your ass don't know shit so don't question me."

"I don't know much about this shit but don't be talking to me like I'm some green ass nigga. I know you missing the meeting wasn't a good impression. Did they tell you about Pops?"

"They didn't tell me shit. They were too fucking busy chewing me up about that petty ass shit that was taken from the trap. What happened though?"

He shook his head and focused on his phone.

Johnazia Gray & Danielle Offett

"You ain't gone tell me?" I asked, moving through traffic.

"They should've told you, man. I'm not trying to overstep my boundaries or no shit like that."

I punched the steering wheel. "This is what the fuck I mean when I say y'all don't treat me like family. How is it that some serious shit is going on and I know nothing about it? What the fuck?"

To be honest, I was over all this shit and I could admit that I was hurt. I knew for a fact that Dom didn't like me and he only put up with me for the sake of Chazae and Semaj, but I didn't know the nigga didn't trust me. I always wanted that father figure that Dom showed those two niggas. When I was younger, he always included me. Now, he treated me like a buster ass nigga which was cool.

"Dom has an open case, man. The feds are watching him," Semaj said, lightening my mood.

"Nooooo, you lying man."

"Real shit. Shit is not looking good, my nigga, so don't fuck up because they're going to have their eyes on everyone in our circle."

That was another reason why I fucked with Semaj. Even when Chazae had his ass on his shoulders, that little nigga would still look out for me and keep me in the loop. He treated me more like a brother then Chazae and that nigga was supposed to be my man's fifty-grand.

"Damn, thanks for that information, bro."

"Aye, check this shit out. I bought this for Derria. You like it?" I almost wrecked when the ring that he showed me almost blinded my eyes. I knew he didn't pay for that shit.

"You want to marry the bitch?" I asked him.

"What I tell you about that, nigga? Don't be calling my wife a bitch." He frowned.

I chuckled and put my hands up in mock surrender.

"Yeah, I want to marry her. You like the ring or not, nigga?"

"I mean, it's straight. Looks cheap," I joked.

He chuckled and waved me off. "Hating ass nigga," he mumbled and I shrugged.

My phone vibrated and flashed letting me know that I had received a text message. When I unlocked my phone, I saw that it was Chazae. I clicked on the message and almost ran the car off the road.

"What the fuck, man? If you need me to drive just say that," Semaj argued, making sure his seatbelt was secure.

Looking at the picture message of the screenshot that Chazae had sent me of him and Shunta's conversation had me choked up. Shunta clearly stated in the messages that she wasn't pregnant and she hadn't seen me in the past few days. I could've kicked my own ass for not being careful and putting Shunta's dumb ass up on game. I read Chazae's message over repeatedly and I knew this nigga was on to my ass.

BRO: So we lyin' now? I been peeping that fuck shit you on, nigga. But if I find out that you're on my pops case or if you had anything to do with that trap getting hit, you're a dead man walking and that's on everything I love, BROTHER.

I shook my head and stuffed my phone in my pocket. Some way and somehow I had to get the heat off of my ass because Chazae was obviously two steps ahead of me.

"Fuck!" I mumbled.

"The fuck is wrong now?"

"Stay out of a grown man's business and bring your in love ass on," I told him.

I wasn't even in the mood for the meeting anymore so I hoped that whatever Lance had to say, he made the shit quick. The second I put my hands on Shunta's ignorant ass, the better I'd probably feel.

I walked into the warehouse with Semaj in tow and greeted all the men that was working for me and Lance. They were some pretty solid niggas and all they cared about was getting money. None of them where involved in the hit that was put on the trap. My cousins were the only ones who knew about that. That was strictly between us. I didn't need Semaj to know anything. I just wanted his little ass to work. He wasn't too good to not get that shit off the muscle, and I didn't understand why Chazae made it like he was just too good for this shit. He was gone learn to be a man.

Lance walked into the building with the rest of my cousins and I was glad. The sooner this shit was over the better. I had a fucking headache as I sat there and thought about all the shit that had happened. Not only did my dumb ass hit my own trap and have to pay the shit back with my money, but Chazae had caught me red handed in a bold face lie. I had to think of something better to tell him because the last thing I needed was to look like I was on some creep shit.

"What's good, my boy?" Me and Lance slapped hands.

"Ain't shit, man. Let's get this meeting started so I can go. Shit's been rough today," I told him.

"You know this nigga?" Lance pointed at Semaj.

"What am I missing?" I asked in an irritated tone.

"Little nigga was at my baby mama house showing off his little toy gun and shit like he was ready to do something," Lance said.

"And I'm still strapped, nigga. What's the difference from then and today?" Semaj snarled, mugging the fuck out of Lance.

"Who your baby mama?" I asked him.

"Dola," Lance answered.

Now I felt like this nigga was trying to get here on a whole other motive. He never once mentioned that his baby mama lived here and I damn sure didn't know that she had any connections with Semaj. This was definitely not supposed to be in the plan.

"Man, listen, this my little brother. He's off limits at all times so gone ahead and throw whatever problem you got with him out the window. He's just my runner and he's here to get money. You hear me?"

I wasn't on the bullshit. Period. I meant it when I said Semaj was off limits.

"Oh, he just a runner. Little pretty boy ass nigga ain't even getting no real money." Lance chuckled.

"Don't really need this money to be honest, my nigga. Do your research." Semaj winked, pissing Lance off even more.

"Shut up, Semaj." I pushed him.

"Start the meeting, man," I told Lance.

"What's up, man? I'm just here showing my face and letting you niggas know who's running this shit." He looked back at Semaj who was laughing and clearly taking him for a joke. "In the streets, never call me by my first name. Call me Dope. I won't be seeing y'all niggas too much because I'll be busy as fuck, but I don't mind popping up. I'm not a sensitive ass nigga, I don't do handouts, and if shit come up missing I kill first and I don't ask questions later. My cousin right here is my right hand so whatever he says pretty much goes. That's it for now."

"All right, meeting adjourned. Head back to your spots," I told all of my workers.

"Keep that little nigga close to you because he bound to get it." Lance sent shooting signals at Semaj before walking off.

Once we got to the car, I broke shit down to Semaj on what his job would consist of.

"I'm not working under that nigga. Period," Semaj said

"Man, you ain't working for him. You working for me," I corrected.

"Let that nigga know not to say shit to me, man. For real. I don't know much about this game but you know I'm far from being a pussy nigga."

"I hear you, man. Am I taking you to your crib or back to Biggs house? I got to go to the projects and handle some shit."

"Nah, drop me off over there. I'ma kick it with Derria and Ms. Shirley."

I nodded my head. I needed a few shots of Hennessy and a fat ass blunt of loud to take this pressure off my back. I had to keep Lance and Semaj away from each other at all times.

CHAPTER NINE

DOLA

"Sissy, I got your stripper heels!" Ri Ri yelled, letting herself into my crib as usual.

I rolled my eyes and opened my bedroom door, knowing she was making her way back. She was being loud and chipper while I was nervous and pulling my hair out. It was going on seven in the evening and I had already redone my hair five times. I was going out with Chazae, yes, Chazae and my stomach was in knots. On one hand, I wanted to say no and keep my guard up but he caught me off guard when he tracked me down in front of my building and made me agree to go out with him.

Oh wait, let him tell it "It's not a date. We're just going out to kick shit."

The other day, his crazy ass parked his car behind mine and wouldn't let me leave without saying yes. It wasn't a coincidence that he knew where I lived. It had to be Semaj and Derria's wanna be cupid looking asses.

"Bitch, I know Chazae would love to see all of that ass, but why are you not dressed?" she asked, looking over my naked body and plopping down on the bed.

I ignored her and went right back to my vanity mirror to play with my hair. I was sitting in front of the mirror in nothing but a black thong and matching bra but at least I had my outfit already ready for me on the bed. I blamed her for not having my shoes back to me last week like I told her.

Johnazia Gray & Danielle Offett

"I don't know what to do with all this damn hair." I complained, growing frustrated. My curls were all over the place and I just wanted it to work with me for one night and allow me to put it into a bun.

The sound of Derria laughing made me turn around in my chair. "What's funny?"

"You." She said, throwing a pair of socks at my head. "It's so cute that you're nervous. First you acted like you didn't want him, now look at you, all nervous and blushing. Just make sure you name your kids after me and Semaj."

"Girl, bye. It's not even that deep. I'm only going because his crazy ass threatened to kidnap me if I didn't agree to go. I swear I got the wrong brother because Chazae is crazy and rude as fuck."

"Aww stop it, Sissy. He's not that bad. A little rough around the edges but he's still a good guy. Y'all have a lot in common you know."

I looked at her and went back to doing my hair.

"Y'all both act so hard but deep down, both all y'all want is love."

I could see her smiling from ear to ear from the mirror. She must've been thinking about her and Semaj because that's the only fairy tale relationship I've witnessed. One too many times I had my heart broken and sometimes by the same nigga. I was straight on the love tip but I wouldn't deny that Chazae didn't have me intrigued.

"Whatever you say, Maya Angelou. Help me get my slim thick ass into this dress. He said be ready by eight so he'll be here any minute now."

Johnazia Gray & *Danielle Offett*

It didn't take long to slip into my little black lace dress. The V-neck gave my boobs the extra push they needed to sit up perfectly and turned this simple dress into an all-purpose fuck me on the kitchen counter dress. It stopped right above my knees just in case we were going somewhere with class. I was a woman of all trades and could fit in anywhere.

"Now go ahead and top it off with them stripper heels." Derria teased.

"Don't try me. You know my work shoes are nothing but six inches or higher." I corrected, slipping into the five-inch stiletto pumps that had a strap going across both sides.

Before I could stand up, I could hear banging on the door. I knew damn well he wasn't banging on my door like the police. He was about to get cursed out in two point five seconds. Making my way to the door Derria was right on my heels. The closer we got, yelling could be heard from the opposite side. Derria and I looked at each other curiously. I shrugged my shoulders and snatched the door open.

"How you gone disrespect me like this, Chazae? You so foul!" Ashlee yelled, hands on her hips.

Chazae, rubbed his hand over his head and ignored her. I didn't know how long they had been arguing but by the way his jaw clenched I could tell he was over it. I felt like I just walked into an episode of Maury.

"These are for you." He said, attempting to pass me a bouquet of roses. Instead, I eyed them and looked from him to Ashlee.

"Chazae, I'm not with the drama shit so go ahead and take your little Chihuahua and gone about y'all business because clearly I'm missing something."

His face turned into a scowl as he mugged Ashlee. "Hell naw, ain't shit to miss. This broad is dizzy as fuck. I already told you she gave me some head and that was it. Derria take ya girl on somewhere."

"Oh, so you gone talk about me like I'm not right here?" Ashlee screamed, getting in his face.

"Ashlee, I told you to stay in the car. You know my sister don't like you." Derria pointed out, grabbing her by the arm only for her to snatch away. "She was just leaving, sis."

I just had a talk with this bitch at Dom's house and from what I heard, this was a one sided situationship. Joking or not, I told her ass to keep it moving and it was clear she didn't take heed to my warning. Chazae wasn't my man but I felt as though she was disrespecting me by coming to my shit and trying to start some mess.

"What are you doing at my door, Ashlee?" I asked her calmly. "He made it clear that your mouth is no longer needed. Move around li'l thotty."

She chucked. "Says the stripper bitch!"

I took a step towards her and Derria squeezed her way in the middle. Since Derria was shorter than the both of us, I sized Ashlee up and immediately knew she didn't want these problems.

"Shawty, are you slow, dumb, or just fucking retarded? Take yo ass on somewhere!" Chazae snapped.

"No! I'm tired of you playing me to the left. I might have a few miles on me but at least I don't let the world see me naked. Ha! You really want to front on me for a stripper bi-"

Before she could finish saying something she would regret, I fired off on her and punched her dead in the mouth. She stumbled backwards and fell onto the floor. Blood flew from her busted lip as she screamed.

"Dayyyuuuum!" Chazae boosted, cupping his hand around his mouth. "Dola, bring yo ass on! The fuck is wrong with y'all?"

"Fuck you! I'm not going nowhere with yo hoe ass. Pick yo bitch up and get the fuck away from my door!" I yelled.

He rubbed his hand over his head. "Aight, Say less."

Unexpectedly, he picked me up like I only weighed ten pounds and walked down the stairs. I kicked and screamed but he wasn't fazed at all. I even threatened his life but he kept it pushing until he had me in the car with the child lock on with his childish ass. As bad as I wanted to be mad at him, it was kind of turning me on.

*****

"So you just gone sit there and be mad at a nigga?" he asked, not even looking up as he sucked the juice from a crab leg.

Since we pulled up to The Crazy Lobster, one of my favorite restaurants, I made sure to give him the silent treatment. Being the rude ass nigga that he was, he didn't even acknowledge my silence. He had already downed three Bourbon Street Tea's, which was made of vodka and coke and now he was demolishing the Lobster Tower entrée. This meal came with two pounds of lobster, snow crab clusters, boiled shrimp, oysters on the half shell, clams, and mussels. His greedy ass was determined to eat every bit.

"Me? Mad? Nah? That's for your bitch to do." I replied, nonchalantly while taking a bite of my stuffed lobster.

Johnazia Gray & *Danielle Offett*

Slurping sound could be heard as he sucked the buttery juices from a shell. I tried not to cream my panties as I watched his sexy ass lick the shell. *Damn, if he could work the tongue on a shell like that, I wonder what else he can do with it*, I thought to myself.

"You must wanna be my bitch then?" he asked sporting a cocky grin.

I sucked my teeth and rolled my eyes, he was definitely feeling himself because I wasn't even thinking about becoming his bitch. Instead of answering him, I leaned across the table to grab a shrimp off his plate. He slapped my hand with a quickness.

I looked up and he had the cutest mug on his face.

"Nah, lil mama. You wanted shrimp, you should've ordered it. Don't be grabbing shit from over here."

"You so damn rude! I only wanted one." I pouted.

"Well, go to the kitchen and see if you can order just one shrimp then."

I rolled my eyes and picked at my meal.

Chazae sucked his teeth and grunted in annoyance. "Here, man."

He scooted his plate in my direction and I gladly picked a few pieces of shrimp off his plate. I smiled so bright you would've thought he just gave me the golden ticket.

"I guess you're not so sour after all." I sucked the shrimp seductively and as expected, his eyes zoned in on my lips.

"I'm not that bad. You just don't like to cut a nigga no slack."

Johnazia Gray & *Danielle Offett*

"Cut you some slack for what? So, you can play me like you do Ashlee? Nah, I'll pass playboy."

He chuckled and took a sip of his tea.

"What's funny?" I asked.

"You're just as dizzy as that girl if you think I'm on some lame ass shit like that. You might not know it, matter of fact, you know just like I know that I'm a boss. If I just wanted to *wam-bam* you I would've asked for the pussy at the door. Don't insult me like that, Ma."

Damn, for the first time, I felt bad for my slick ass mouth. He really sounded sincere and looked like he was hurt by me calling him out. I knew he could fuck any bitch he wanted but for some reason, he was out with me. Don't get it twisted, I could have any nigga I wanted to wine and dine me too but for some reason here we were.

"Sorry." I told him sincerely.

"You good. You just not used to a real nigga like me. Tell me something I don't know about Ms. Dola besides she got a fly mouth and got a mean right hook."

We both laughed. Just that quick, I forgot about the part of me knocking Ashlee in her shit. She deserved it and I would do it again if I needed to. I never liked her so it wasn't about Chazae. It was about me waiting on a reason to give her a taste of these hands.

"You're too cute to be fighting with women like Ashlee."

I turned my head a little to hide my blush. Chazae, the rude and cocky man in front of me thought I was cute.

"It's just something about her I don't like. I've only tolerated her for Derria's sake, but I'd knock her out a million more times if that's what it takes for Derria to see that Ashlee is as fake as that ass on her."

Chazae choked on his drink. "You hell for that."

We made small talk as I told him about my slim to none family members and why I was so protective of Derria. I even told him about being a single mother raising Princess. Unlike most men, he actually seemed interested and asked questions. He opened up a bit about his mom and how proud he was of Semaj. I rested my head on my hands and smiled as we bragged on Semaj and his accomplishments. Some people didn't like for others to succeed, family or not. I could tell by the passionate look in his eyes that he would do anything to make sure his brother was straight. That's the same way I felt about Derria and her finishing school. Damn, I guess Derria's cupid ass was right. We did have a lot in common.

"Why you staring at me with that goofy smile on your face?" he asked, smiling back at me.

I didn't even notice I was staring at him. "Boy ain't nobody staring. I'm just happy to hear about your family. Honestly, I'm shocked to be having such a good time with you."

He put his hand over his heart. "Damn, I'm hurt."

"Aww, I'm just being honest. Seriously, I don't hang out much outside of work so thanks. Next outing on me."

"Oh, so you're planning another date already?"

"I thought this wasn't a date?" I asked, remembering him specifically telling me we were kicking shit.

He laughed. "Well, if I'm paying for your meal without even getting the pussy, this is definitely a date."

I threw a piece of bread at him. "If you wanted some pussy, that's all you had to say." I licked my lips before sipping my drink.

This was only a test but the look in his eyes was of pure lust. I would be lying if I said, my panties weren't drenched or that I didn't have a mini orgasm by just looking at him.

"Check please." He called out.

He didn't even wait for the ticket before placing three crisp, hundred dollar bills in our waiter's hand. "Keep the change."

The waiter smiled and ran off like Ashton Kutcher was going to pop out and tell him he had been punked.

He stood up and shifted his stiff member. "Let me get you home before I end up bending your little ass over the table. I'm trying to be a gentleman."

What if I don't want you to be a gentleman, I thought to myself. Instead of saying it out loud, I smiled and walked in front of him. My hips swayed a little more than usual just for him. I was on a cloud as he drove me home. Even though I came out just to get him out of my hair. I had to admit that he was growing on me. In my head, I was secretly excited about my next date with rude ass Chazae.

CHAPTER TEN

SEMAJ

"How come you didn't hire somebody to do this shit, nigga? Got me in here working like a bitch," Chazae cursed, causing me to laugh.

Today was the day that I was going to propose to Derria and a nigga was working full time in this room. I reserved a suite at the Royal Sonesta Hotel for the weekend. I had my brother in here helping me with the rose petals and decorations and we were doing good. We didn't need no damn decorators.

"We almost finished, nigga. I just need to fill the tub up with some rose petals. You like the gifts and shit?" I asked him.

I had spent a little over five thousand dollars buying Derria all the things she liked. She had new Pandora bracelets, brand new glasses from the Gucci and Prada store, and every expensive heel you could think of, she had it. Of course, I had to decorate the room with dozens of roses since those were her favorite. I really wasn't ashamed of shit. I was happy with Derria and it was my plan to give her and show her the world.

"I'm proud of you, little nigga. I think Derria is an amazing girl for you. Just never do nothing to push her to being a bad girl because once her ass is bad, she ain't never going back. You hear me?"

I laughed and nodded.

"Tell me something, bruh. You don't think I'm moving too fast?" I asked him.

"What did Pops tell you?"

Johnazia Gray & *Danielle Offett*

"Pops don't think I'm moving fast at all. He's on some 'love ain't got no time limit on it' type shit."

"And I agree. Shit, if you love her the way you do, why not put a ring on it? You might as well before somebody else does."

I nodded my head.

"What's up with you and Dola?"

He smiled and waved me off. "I fuck with her. I have to keep my distance though. I know she'll have a nigga trying to propose and shit like your ass is doing and I don't know if I'm ready for all that just yet. I took her out the other night and I had to take her ass home because I was ready to fuck her right there in the restaurant."

"She's a good chick. I fuck with her. You met her daughter?"

"Nah, she told me she allow no man around her daughter unless she know for a fact that was going to be her man, and I respect that."

"I'm glad to hear y'all doing good. Who knows? You may be her man soon." I punched him in the arm.

Chazae seemed to be a little down about something.

"What's wrong, bruh?" I asked him.

"Dom has been talking like he know he's fixing to go away for a long time and that shit is killing me. What I'ma do if they take my old man? He all I got besides you."

"Man, Dom ain't going nowhere. He got some of the biggest fucking lawyers behind him. We gone be good and don't be talking all down and shit. Y'all haven't heard nothing about who's on the case?"

"Nope. We're just waiting."

I took a look over the room and turned off the lights when we were getting ready to head out.

"I see you and Tauris been spending a lot of one on one time together too. What's good with that?" Chazae asked, staring a hole through me.

"Ain't shit good. That's our nigga. I just been feeling a little sorry for that nigga," I lied.

"You lying but I'll find out later. I don't really like getting you involved with shit that deals with the game, Semaj, but Tauris is up to no good. Stay away from that nigga, for real, man. He's my best friend and I haven't even been fucking with him."

My gut told me to bring up Tauris running his own operation but I couldn't do that. He wasn't hurting nobody and I knew he wouldn't cross my family. I just felt that nigga needed the love Chazae and I was getting from our father. He wasn't used to that and honestly they didn't make him feel like family how they were supposed to.

"I think y'all tripping. He's just lost, man. That's all. The nigga ain't never really had nobody but us and his grandma. He ain't on no foul shit."

"Semaj, you don't know shit, man. You don't know Tauris how I know Tauris. I know that nigga more than he know himself. Stay away from him until I figure shit out, okay?"

"All right, man." I lied.

No way was I falling back from Tauris. That was my brother too and I was getting some major bread running with that nigga so far. The shit wasn't hard at all and I was always safe. I enjoyed working by his side. Nobody had to know but the two of us.

*****

Johnazia Gray & *Danielle Offett*

"Everything looks perfect, Pops. I appreciate this, man," I thanked my father.

Dom was the best, man. He had gone out of his way to prepare a dinner and make the house look romantic for the proposal. Everything you could think of was on the menu and I couldn't wait until we all could dig in. Dom got all of his cooking skills from Charae and he sure as hell used them. It wasn't nothing that he couldn't make and Derria loved his cooking.

"Wait right here, son. I got something for you." He wiped his hands on his apron.

I looked at Chazae and shook my head. Dom was full of surprises.

"How you feeling, bruh?" Chazae asked me.

"I'm nervous as fuck. What if I'm all excited and her ass says no?"

"If she say no, shoot a nigga."

We laughed together.

I couldn't lie. I was looking forward to Ms. Shirley and Dola too. They had helped me as much as they could with planning this engagement and I couldn't thank them enough. Even though Ms. Shirley wanted to come and help my old man make all Derria's favorites, Dola talked her out of it. I loved their asses like they were a part of me.

"Give her this one," my father said, handing me a small box.

When I opened it, my mouth dropped. The ring was beautiful as fuck and it made mine look like shit.

"Wait, that's the same ring that Charae used to have," Chazae said, snatching the box out of my hand.

"That's right. That's not the same one, but I got it made exactly like that. What y'all think?" Dom smiled.

It was no secret that he was still in love with Charae, even not being in contact with each other and not having any kind of communication. I always loved Charae and I didn't judge her for the things she did and the career she chose. Chazae was the one with the problem. Charae looked out for me in the most motherly way possible. I loved her ass and I knew Dom wasn't the same without her. To make him happy, that was the ring I was going to give my girl.

"You're still in love with her snake ass, man." Chazae frowned and shook his head.

"Aye, what I tell you about disrespecting your mama?" Dom frowned.

"Fuck her." He waved Dom off and handed me the box.

When Dom sighed and shook his head, I knew he was ready to knock Chazae out.

"I love it. Hopefully me and Derria will have some shit like you and Charae had back then, man." I closed the box and put it in my pocket.

"Me and y'all mama was something special, man. I just wish it was shit I could change." Dom looked sad.

"Then you would've been married to a pig. Everything happens for a reason, Daddy." Chazae bit his banana.

"Now ain't the time for this conversation. Derria and the rest of them just pulled up," I told them.

Dom snatched off his apron and took it to the laundry room. The door was unlocked and Dola knew to just walk straight in.

Johnazia Gray & *Danielle Offett*

"Oh my God, Dola! You can't just walk in Mr. Dom's house without knocking. That's rude," I heard Derria going off on her sister.

When they turned the corner and walked into the dining room area, Derria stopped dead in her tracks with her mouth opened wide. Me, my father, and Semaj were standing by our chairs in our tuxes with smiles on our faces. Derria probably thought that it was just a romantic dinner for all of us, but this was specifically for her.

The lights were dimmed low and all around the room were beautiful heart candles and roses just how it was back at the room. She was in for something big tonight.

"Oh my goodness. Did y'all do this for us?" Derria covered her mouth.

"It looks so nice in here. I'm surprised you ain't need my damn help." Ms. Shirley smiled.

"Be respectful, Ma," Princess said, squeezing Ms. Shirley's hand.

"You're right, baby." She kneeled down and kissed Princess' head.

I looked over at Chazae who was eyeing Dola down. The ladies looked good as fuck and I didn't blame him for eye fucking the shit out of her. I knew that Dola didn't want her daughter around Chazae as of yet, but Princess couldn't miss the engagement and Dola had no problems with it when I brought it to her attention.

"Ladies, have a seat." My father smiled.

He and Ms. Shirley sat at the head of the table while Derria sat next to me and Dola. Chazae and Princess sat next to each other.

Johnazia Gray & Danielle Offett

After my father blessed the food, we all got engaged in some good conversation while we passed the dishes back and forward to one another.

"God must've answered my prayers because I was just telling Dola and Ma Shirley how I wanted some of my favorite foods to eat," Derria said, digging in.

"It smells good. I got to taste it and make sure it taste good though," Ms. Shirley teased my father and winked.

"If it ain't good, shoot me, Ms. Shirley." He laughed.

"I tell you, Dola and Chazae sure do make a nice couple don't they?" Derria smiled.

"They sure do. I keep telling Dola that's a keeper right there." Ms. Shirley smiled.

"Let's not make this about me and Chazae." Dola blushed.

"Why can't we?" He smiled. If I wasn't mistaken, my boy was secretly in love over there.

"Mommy, is this your boyfriend that you're always talking to on the phone?" Princess asked.

"No, P, that's my friend."

"He looks better than my daddy," she said, causing Derria to burst out and laugh.

"Oh, God." Dola dropped her head.

Everyone joined Derria with the laugh.

"Where Tauris at, Semaj?" Chazae asked me in front of everyone.

"Hmm…" Derria rolled her eyes.

"I keep telling that nigga, man." My father shook his head and ate his steak.

I had invited Tauris to come to the dinner for the proposal but the nigga didn't show up. I know that he and Chazae hadn't been on the best of terms so that's probably why he didn't want to come. Shit, he was always complaining about how he didn't feel like family and shit so I would've felt wrong if I didn't invite him.

I didn't invite Ashlee because that bitch wasn't a real friend to my baby. She was just going to have to catch the action off of social media or some shit.

After everyone finished their food, I stood and took Derria by her hand.

"Everyone is looking at us, Semaj." She blushed.

"Let them look." I bent down on one knee catching her completely off guard.

When she looked at everyone and saw their phones out recording, tears fell from her eyes.

"Derria, since you've been in my life, I've been the happiest young nigga I could ever be."

"Watch your mouth," Ms. Shirley said.

"Ma!" Dola slightly tapped Shirley's arm.

"You've motivated me in so many ways and I love you for it. You're smart, you're beautiful, and you're an all-around awesome and genuine person. I really don't want to spend my life with nobody other than you. We have one more semester to go before we get these degrees and it's only right that you rock my last name when they call you on that stage to receive it. So what you say?"

"Yes, baby. Of course." She broke down and started crying. I slipped the ring on her finger and kissed her lips.

"Yayyyyyy! Go, Auntie!" Princess ran and jumped in her arms.

"I'm so happy for y'all." Dola wiped her tears and hugged the both of us.

"I raised a man." My father hugged me.

"Congratulations, bruh." Me and Chazae slapped hands and hugged.

"I approve this. I'm so happy for y'all." Ms. Shirley hugged and kissed the both of our cheeks.

For the remainder of the night at my father's house, we listened to some jazz and had conversation until I was ready to surprise my baby with what I had planned for her back at the room. She was so excited as I watched her take a million pictures of her ring and post it on Snapchat and Instagram.

"All right, me and my wife gone get out of here. Thank y'all so much for everything," I thanked them.

*****

I put the blind fold over Derria's eyes before we walked into the suite.

"You ready?" I asked her.

"Yes, baby. I am." She nodded.

We walked into the room and I took the blindfold off.

"Semaj." She started crying, "What did I do to deserve you?" She kissed me and hugged me tight.

"Nah, more like what I did to deserve you, pretty girl."

She walked over to the bed and scanned through all of her gifts.

"Oh my God, these shoes are bad as hell. How much did you pay for all of this?"

"Don't worry about that, ma. Don't ever worry about the price of nothing with me. You get what you want and deserve." She blushed.

"Did my sister help you decorate this room?"

"Nah, actually me and Chazae worked full time in this bitch. We had to watch a few YouTube videos, but aye, it turned out nice."

She laughed. "I bet Chazae was talking shit the whole time."

"He said I should've hired someone, but overall that nigga enjoyed helping me." I laughed.

After helping her take all of the gifts off the bed and into the corner, I watched her as she stripped butt naked out of her clothes. The sight of her body had a nigga dick on rock hard and I was ready to get a piece of that.

"Come here." She motioned with her finger and lay back on the bed.

When she spread her legs and slowly rubbed on her clit, my mouth watered. Her pussy was beautiful and I just wanted to kiss it.

I pinned her legs back a little further then slid my tongue all around her clit and her opening.

"Oh, shit," she moaned.

I was the first nigga to get inside of that and I was definitely going to be the last.

I flicked my tongue from her pussy to her ass and she was going crazy.

"Oh my God, bae!" she screamed.

"You like that shit, Derria??" I asked her.

She moaned and nodded. With tears escaping her eyes, I knew she was about to reach her climax. After freeing myself from my boxers, I leaned up and slowly pushed my dick inside of her. It still felt like the first time. Tight, warm, and extremely wet.

We fucked for what seemed to be hours until we had no energy left. I lay there in bed with her body under mine and kissed her neck.

"I love you, ma," I told her.

"I love you too, baby. Besides my sister and Ms. Shirley, you're like the best thing that has ever happened to me."

"The feelings are mutual, man. I can't even explain how much I love you."

"Semaj, can I say something and I don't want to ruin the mood."

"Speak your mind."

"Whatever you've gotten yourself into with Tauris needs to come to an end, immediately. I notice how much you're in the hood now and I also notice how much time you spend with him. I know you more than you think I do, and I don't want you involved in that kind of mess. What you want to be in the streets for anyway, Semaj? You're good on money."

"Yeah, on my pops and brother money. Not my own money, Derria."

It was pride that put me into the game, but I really didn't like the fact that I was being taken care of. I was a grown ass man.

"Then take the money your pops and brother give you and start a business. I'm not marrying you if you continue this. I'm in love with a school boy. Not a drug dealer. I don't want you in the mix of that. I love you too much to lose you, baby."

"You're right, ma. I'll put an end to it, but tell me something. Why you never mentioned it before now?"

"I was going to. I just didn't know you were going to propose to me, but since you did I had to get that out there."

I nodded my head.

"And Tauris isn't your friend. Remember that."

I didn't even comment. I just gripped her tight in my arms and we both went to sleep.

I'd get out soon, but right now the money was too good.

CHAPTER ELEVEN

CHAZAE

I shrugged my shoulders causing Dola's head to fall off. "Girl, getcho big ass head off of me. You know that shit gains ten pounds when you sleep." I rotated my arm to stretch it out. "Damn, I think you broke my shit."

Dola grabbed the pillow from off her lap and attempted to slap me with it, but I was quicker than her and slapped it away.

"Shut up! I wasn't even sleep. I was just laying here thinking."

We had been chilling together for the past few weeks against my better judgment. Shit, I told myself I was gone stay away from her but she was really cool peoples. After the engagement dinner, Derria and Semaj had pretty much abandoned us. Somehow, we ended up finding comfort in each other. We weren't hanging out on a clingy tip but I would be lying if I didn't admit enjoying her company. Her little ass was really growing on a nigga.

I was an observant nigga so after a few weeks, I could tell it was something on her mind. Any other bitch I wouldn't have cared to know, but Dola wasn't just any bitch. I pulled her closer to me and ran my fingers through her hair.

"Sit next to Daddy and tell me what's wrong," I told her.

"You're so damn silly but it's not nothing bad. I was just thinking about Semaj and Derria. It was so beautiful to watch him propose to her. I'm just so happy and proud of them."

I could see the love in her eyes when she spoke. She pulled out her phone and started to go through some of the pictures we took of them that night. Those were some nice pictures but I was tired of looking after the first ten.

"If you don't getcho ole' grandma ass out of here. Pulling up old baby pictures and shit," I joked.

She laughed and tossed her phone on the table.

"I'm being serious. Damn, my little sister is going to get married before me. I damn near raised her little cute ass. Can you believe it?"

The way she looked at me caused me to shift in my seat. Was she hinting at marriage because that shit was not in the cards for us no time soon. I fucked with her heavy but not that damn heavy. I tried to find the right words to break her down easily. I didn't want to feed her no fairy tale shit when I knew damn well it wasn't happening. Shit, I had groceries older than our friendship. Fuck no.

"Look, I fuck with you but marriage–"

She burst out laughing. "Boy, save your little speech. I don't want to marry your ass either. It was just a simple statement. Over there sweating like a stripper, lighten up!"

I wiped the imaginary sweat off my forehead. "Woah! You had a nigga scared for a minute. I ain't even get to Donald Trump yo' ass and you wanna marry a nigga."

"What the fuck is Donald Trumping?" she asked, raising her eye brow.

"I'm saying, I didn't even get to grab you by the pussy yet."

This time, she hit me with the pillow and I wasn't able to block it.

"Now I see where Semaj gets his disrespectful ass comments from because it sure ain't come from Dom. You so damn disrespectful," she snapped, rolling her eyes and leaning away from me.

Using my hand, I swiped her face in attempt to wipe the frown off her pretty face.

"Come on now, ma. You know I was just fucking with you. Get outcha feelings."

She rolled her eyes and went to grab her phone. I jumped up and snatched it off the table.

"Go get me a banana first and I'll think about giving you your phone back."

She looked at me like I had her fucked up but I didn't give a fuck. I didn't feel like walking to the kitchen and I knew how women were about their phones, so I knew she would get up and get it.

"Excuse me? Give me my damn phone. Do I look like a maid? I'm not going to get shit."

She reached for it but I moved it away. Just like I thought, she rolled her eyes and stormed off to the kitchen. Not even a minute later, she returned with a banana.

"Good girl." I threw the phone toward her and surprisingly she caught it with one hand. "Now hand over the banana."

She smiled and took a step back. I knew she wasn't about to play with me like that.

"Don't do it, Dola," I warned, reading her mind.

One peel at a time, she uncovered the banana. Before I could warn her again, she bit into the banana and closed her eyes like it was a juicy steak and she was savoring the butter.

"Don't be a baby. Here." She reached in her back pocket and threw me a banana. "What's up with you and fruit anyway?" she asked, taking another bite.

I smiled and licked my lips at the dirty thoughts going through my head. "I just love fruit. Gotta keep my kids healthy, ya feel me."

"You got kids too?" she asked, looking in my direction.

Once she noticed the boyish grin on my face, she rolled her eyes.

"You're so damn nasty."

I winked at her. "I'm trying to get nasty with you."

It was the half-truth. I never waited for pussy in my life. Never had to wait for it or ask for it. Up until now, I wasn't pressed to have sex with Dola but the way she was eating that banana had me wanting to fuck like a teenage boy. I wasn't pressed so if she wasn't feeling it yet, it was no pressure. We talked about sex and I already knew, just like me, she was guarded. I was a nigga so I fucked and ducked to keep my guard up but her being a woman, she had to guard that pussy with her life. I respected that.

She played with her fingers. "You already know how I feel about that, Zae."

I knew she was uncomfortable and that was the last thing I wanted.

"I know. I was just fucking with you."

She tooted her lips. "So, you don't want to have sex with me?"

I chuckled. "Hell yeah I want to fuck yo' little cute ass, but I understand you ain't ready for that."

Her eyes lowered as she licked her juicy lips. As she made her way directly in front of me, my dick jumped on its own. Leaning forward, she forcefully yanked my head to the side. I could feel her breath getting closer to my neck.

"This your spot, babe?" she whispered in my ear.

Johnazia Gray & *Danielle Offett*

I felt like a little bitch for feeling a tingling sensation in my body. That neck licking shit was going to make me tear her little ass up. Then suddenly, instead of a tongue, I felt her teeth clamping down on my neck. My eyes shot open and I tried to move away but it was too late because she already locked down like a Chihuahua.

"Augghhhh! Shit!" I roared.

She let go of my neck and allowed her head to fall back while she laughed.

"What the fuck is wrong with you?" I asked, rubbing my neck.

"That's for being disrespectful nigga talking about you gon' Donald Trump me."

I looked at her and she stood in front of me laughing her ass off. Even though that shit hurt, I couldn't help but laugh.

"Yeah, aight keep them damn K9 teeth off me."

I yanked her down on my lap and began to tickle her until she laughed uncontrollably. Even when I saw tears coming down her eyes, I didn't stop. She wanted to play around then we were going to play. I loved to hear her beg and plead. It felt good to freely act up with somebody. Once I saw that she had enough, I stopped tickling her and sat her on the couch next to me.

She wiped her tears and attempted to catch her breath.

"We should make this shit official," I blurted out.

Did I just ask her to be my woman? Clearly, I had because it came out of my mouth. It felt like the right moment. Making her my woman had been on my mind ever since I had that talk with Dom. I wanted to stay away but the distance just made me want to be around her even more.

Johnazia Gray & *Danielle Offett*

"I'm not talking marriage or no shit like that, but I want this shit to be official. So, what do you say?"

She sat there, silent. I could tell she was pondering the thought in her head. Was she going to say no? I felt stupid as fuck for bringing it up. I promised myself that I wasn't going to catch feelings for these hoes but Dola was different. She made me think different and want more. Fuck it, I had to ask. If she decided to say no, I would just take it like a man.

"Damn, you ain't gotta do a nigga like that. Just let me know I'm ugly or something," I said, trying to make light of her silence.

"I want to be with you too. I'm just scared," she admitted. "My baby daddy really did some fuck boy shit to me and I don't want to go through that again."

I looked in her eyes and could see all the hurt and pain that lame ass nigga had caused her. She told me how he said he loved her but took her through some crazy shit and dipped. That was some real fuck boy shit and that wasn't in my DNA.

She put her head down and began to play with her fingers.

"Ma, it's a simple question. Are you ready to ride with a nigga?" I asked her.

She looked confused.

"I'm not a nine to five ass nigga. The streets raised me so I'm in the trenches day and night. I'm not gon' give you some fairytale bullshit and tell you everything will be perfect. I'm not gon' say that I'll love you the right way because I don't know how to love. The woman who brought me into this world didn't even love me enough to stay. My head is all fucked up but what I do know is that I am a man of my word, and would never hurt you like that nigga did. We only been chilling for a little bit but

Johnazia Gray & Danielle Offett

you being mine feel right. If you're not ready, it's cool. No pressure at all. We can take this as slow as you want, ma."

"I'm ready to ride but we have to take this slow," she said.

"You sure?" I asked. "Like I said, I know you've been hurt. On top of that, I'm not a regular ass nigga with a regular ass job. I understand if you need time to think. You have a lot to think about."

I needed an honest answer from her. I didn't do this dating shit so if we gave this shit a try and she wasn't in it foreal, then I wouldn't hesitate to end it. I didn't need any fake love around me.

"Let me tell you something. I'm not new to this shit. My baby daddy, Lance, was in the game. So, I know firsthand how the street life goes. I don't ask for much. All I need is honesty, loyalty, and openness. If you can give me that I'll ride with you until the wheels fall off."

Damn, my li'l baby was a rider too? Before I could respond, my phone went off. It was my work phone so I had no choice but to answer it.

"What?" I asked, irritated.

"Sorry to bother you, Boss, but we need you to come to the spot on Plank Road. Niggas just came through with the water guns. It's hot outchea," Young Rolo, one of my workers said.

"Where the fuck is Tauris?" I yelled. He should've been checking the spots and holding shit down. He was supposed to be *on call* for shit like this. I was the backup contact.

"Shit, last I heard he said he had to take a business trip so he dipped out last night," Rolo informed me.

I hung up on him without saying another word.

I moved Dola off my lap and began to put my shoes on. This was the shit I was talking about. He was moving all wrong.

When did we start taking business trips without saying shit? I damn sure didn't have any meetings on my calendar so what business did he have to tend to? Because he wanted to move in silence, some shit popped off in his territory, once again, and I had to go fix it.

"Zae, is everything okay?" Dola asked, rubbing my shoulder. I was so fucking thrown off that I forgot she was sitting there. I could read the worry on her face.

I stood up and kissed her on her forehead.

"Yeah, nothing for your beautiful ass to worry about. I just gotta go handle some shit. Stay here and be naked on my bed when I get back," I told her before grabbing my keys and walking out the door.

"Be careful!" I heard her yell.

My mind was racing. My gut was telling me that some shit wasn't right with Tauris but I couldn't put my finger on it. I knew he was moving funny and having mood swings, but that wasn't enough to convict him. With Dom being investigated, he was really looking suspect. I needed to see what the fuck was up with him before some shit went down that I couldn't fix.

*****

Pulling up to the trap house, it didn't seem like shit was popping. Majority of the homes were either vacant or rented out by functioning crackheads. Once out the car, I surveyed my surroundings. Nothing was out of place so I walked up to the door. The door was still on the hinges so what could have popped off?

Johnazia Gray & *Danielle Offett*

I dialed Tauris a million times on the way over and each time, his ass didn't answer. I didn't want to worry Pops with this shit. I knew he had enough going on.

I did the secret knock and Rolo came to the door with a mean mug and blood splattered all over his face and shirt. He looked like he had gotten in a fight with a bear and had to slice his neck to survive.

"What the fuck happened?" I asked, walking in and closing the door behind me. I looked around and there were bullet holes in the wall and blood stains on the carpet, but I didn't see any bodies. What the fuck was going on?

Rolo headed to the basement and I followed right behind him. I readjusted the strap on my hip just in case it was some funny shit going on. I couldn't be too trusting with these niggas. Once down the stairs, I almost lost it.

"What the fuck is this shit?" It looked like World War Three had just ended. There was a pile of dead bodies on one side and three workers standing on the other. Only one worker stood out to me because instead of standing with the others, he was tied up and sitting on the floor next to the dead bodies. His name was Trey. From the swollen eyes lids and bruised face, I could tell he had taken an ass whooping before I showed up.

"Start talking," I said to no one in particular. Everyone was quiet as a mouse and I needed to know what the fuck was going on.

"So we in here, working and shit. This nigga, Trey, said he had to make a store run. He comes back thirty minutes later. Did the secret knock and everything so I let him in. I turn to walk away. Next thing we know, like six niggas run up in this bitch blasting!" Rolo said. He went into detail about how the shootout went. Honestly, I didn't give a fuck. What I needed to know was who, why, and how.

"You said six niggas rushed up in here. I only see four dead niggas."

"The other two got away, Boss," one of the other workers, Sino, said, holding his bloodied arm. He was a loyal nigga to be sitting here with a gunshot wound just to show me he wasn't in on shit. I walked over and examined his arm. It was only a flesh wound. He would be okay. I still sent him to our hood doctor to get checked out. We didn't do hospitals for shit we couldn't legally explain.

Once Sino walked out, I turned my attention to Trey. I walked over to him and took the tape off his mouth.

"Damn, Trey. You really moving like that? I remember like yesterday you was getting beat on by your pops while your moms shot that shit up her arm. Who saved you?" I asked him.

He murmured something that was very inaudible.

"I can't hear you, son. Who put you in the game and killed that nigga for you?"

"You did," he said, looking at the ground.

"I know I did. You want to know why? Because I had love for you, my nigga, and this is how you repay me?" I looked at him with anger and disgust. "I'm not going to lie and say I'ma let you live because you know how this shit go, but since you were my little homie, I'ma make it real quick. First, I need for you to tell me why you would cross me. If it was money you needed, I would've blessed you and you know that. So give me a good reason."

He shook his head. I saw a lonely tear escape his eye. At this moment, he knew he fucked up and it was going to cost him his life.

"It wasn't just about the money. I owed this nigga some money and the interest built up so high that he said he didn't want the money anymore. He said all I had to do was let a few of his homies hit this spot and my debt would be paid. I didn't want to do it. I put that on my son I didn't, but he threatened to kill my baby moms if I didn't go through with it. I swear I would never purposely cross you, Zae." He cried.

I shook my head. Niggas acted like they didn't know who the fuck I was. If some niggas had him by the balls and was threatening him, all he had to do was talk to me and I would've had that shit handled. But he wanted to cross a nigga and handle it himself.

"Who's the nigga you owed?" I asked.

"This nigga name Dope. I'm telling you, this nigga is crazy as fuck! He just got in town but he already making moves like he trying to take over."

Dope. Never heard of that nigga but I didn't miss the fact he said this nigga was from out of town. "Where this nigga from?" I asked.

"Chicago, I think."

"He drive a black on black Charger?" I asked, rubbing my goatee.

Trey nodded his head.

"You know where I can find this nigga?" I asked.

"I don't know where that nigga lay his head at but I do know that he has a trap house out in Sherwood. Them shits so low key though so you wouldn't know it was a trap. It's the only house with a red mailbox."

I nodded my head in satisfaction. I already had men looking for this nigga but now that I had a name and a place, I was sure to find him. It was clear that he was looking for me. Guess it was time I paid him a visit.

"Thanks, my man. I'ma go ahead and make sure yo' little nigga straight. Rolo, off this nigga and call Gunz and Smokey to come clean this mess up."

Gunz and Smokey were our duo cleanup crew. They could clean up any mess like it never happened.

I headed back upstairs and out to my car. Once again, Tauris' fuck ass wasn't answering the phone, so I called two of my lieutenants that I knew were solid. I hated to ride out with just anybody but Cash and Big Melo would do. They were twin brothers so I knew they were together.

"Call Cash," I called out to the car.

"Calling Cash," the car repeated.

Unlike Tauris, this nigga picked up on the first ring.

"Wassup, Boss Man. Everything is good over here," he said, getting right to the point.

"That's wassup. I know Melo is with you. I need y'all boys to ride to the Northside with me to Sherwood. We can link up at the QuikTrip."

"Say less," he said before hanging up.

I pressed on the gas doing ninety on the highway. Whoever this nigga Dope was, was causing a lot of drama and for what? I didn't fucking know. This was the second spot he hit and it was time for some repercussions.

I drove like a bat out of hell and got to the gas station in thirty minutes. I didn't even get out the car; I pulled up next to them and let them know we were about to ride out on some niggas. They had their guns locked, loaded, and was ready to ride out. I pulled out first and they followed close by. There was only one neighborhood in Sherwood that I didn't have a trap house in, so this one had to be where he was at and the reason I never ran into this nigga, Dope.

Pulling in the neighborhood, I cruised through. There was no sign of that nigga, Dope or his Charger but I saw a red mailbox up ahead. I smiled at my discovery. I dialed Cash up and put him on speaker.

Sounds of him choking on some fire ass weed could be heard for the first five seconds. "Yo'!"

"You see them niggas sitting on the porch up ahead? The one with the red mailbox?"

"Yeah. Those the niggas?" he asked.

"Yup. Ride up slow and leave a message for me and meet me at the end of the block," I told him before disconnecting the call.

Cash whipped his blue Honda with the tinted windows in front of me. I sat back and watched as they cruised up toward the house. Those niggas sitting on the porch must've been young and dumb because they didn't even see them coming. Cash stopped directly in front of the house and immediately started letting off shots.

The men on the porch tried to take cover and draw their weapons but it was too late. Before they could let off any shots, Cash and Big Melo had already lit their asses up. A few niggas came out the house but were shot on sight. After all the bodies were left on the ground, my men sped off down the street. It was the hood so it was going to take a minute for the police to show, if they ever did.

I gripped the steering wheel in excitement and cruised by to make sure everyone was dead. As I looked around, all were motionless except for one body trying to crawl up the porch. The dude was wearing an all-black jump suit but I knew he was hit because I could see the red blood trailing behind him.

Just the thought of being disrespected made me want to go and see who this nigga was. Since he wanted to fuck with me, I wanted him to see my face before he took his last breath. I hopped out my whip and looked up and down the street. Not a soul came out their houses. I removed the gun from the side of my sweats and crept up on him.

Once I was right behind him, I kicked him in his side. "Turn yo' bitch ass over, nigga!" I barked, ready to blow his brains out.

I could hear the dude mumbling and groaning but couldn't understand what he was saying. Using my foot, I kicked him over on his back so that I could see his face.

Once we made eye contact, I dropped my gun. *What the fuck did I just do?*

"Ch..Cha..Z…Z...Zae?" he said, coughing up blood between syllables.

I dropped down and grabbed him into my arms. "What the fuck, man!" I screamed. "What the fuck are you doing out here, Semaj?"

He tried to speak but only blood came out. "Stop trying to talk! Don't try to fucking talk, man!" I yelled.

In the distance, I saw Cash speeding back up on us. Him and Melo hopped out the car and rushed over to us. Once they saw who I was holding, they rubbed their heads and cursed.

"Don't just stand there, help me get him in the car! Open the fucking car door!" I yelled. I didn't even realize it but tears were streaming down my face. It wasn't a soft cry, it was the snot nose cry that I never experienced before. My heart was hurting.

Semaj's body started to shake uncontrollably. "Don't leave me, baby bro! You can't leave me. I fucked up. I know I did. Just hold on. Just hold on!" I cried, trying to lift him up.

Between his dead weight and me barely being able to move, I was struggling getting him up. I snapped the fuck out as I looked up to see them still standing there.

"Come on! Melo, get your big ass over here and help me!"

"He's gone, Boss," Cash said.

I followed his eyes down to Semaj who was no longer moving. His eyes were wide open and staring directly at me. I knew he was gone.

"No!" I roared, from the pit of my stomach. I cradled him in my arms and rocked back and forth while slapping him in the face repeatedly.

"Nah, you can't go out like that. Come on, man. You're getting married soon and you're gonna finish school. Get up. Die on me and I'll kill you! Get up!"

Using the little bit of energy I had left, I stood up and attempted to drag him to the car.

"Just open the door. He's coming with us."

They looked at me like I was a madman. Suddenly, police sirens could be heard.

"Fuck! I'm sorry, Boss, but we gotta go. Leave him here. Semaj is dead. We gotta get the fuck outta here," Melo yelled, trying to grab Semaj's lifeless body from me

The sirens grew nearer and I could hear Melo and Cash yelling for me to come on.

"Zae, we can't leave you my nigga but you need to come the fuck on!"

I finally snapped out of my daze and kissed Semaj on the forehead.

"I love you, bro. I promise I'm sorry." I took one last look at my little brother's lifeless body before hopping back in my car and speeding off. We turned the corner just in time because police cars were headed in that direction.

In the car, I headed straight to Pops' house. I could barely drive because my hands were shaking so badly, but somehow I managed to make it. Once I made it to his home, I didn't even turn the car off before I jumped out and ran inside. My legs were so weak. I fell once I entered the foyer. I didn't have the energy to get up so I just laid there and continued to cry. I really fucked up this time.

"Pops!" I yelled to the top of my lungs.

Rosa, my father's maid ran to me.

"Oh my goodness, Chazae! Are you okay? Are you bleeding?" she asked, trying to help me up.

I pushed her away from me. "Where the fuck is my Pops?" I yelled, not meaning to take my anger out on her but I was hurting.

"I'm so sorry," Rosa said, looking at me with pity and sadness. "Some people with vests on came here about two hours ago and arrested your father. Said something about him being charged with drug trafficking and some other things I don't understand."

This was too much for me. Not only did my little brother die because of me and the life that I lived, now my father was locked up. My head began to spin out of control. I felt like my life was leaving my body but I didn't care. I just hoped my spirit went to wherever Semaj was. Death would be better than living for me. Before I knew it, all I saw was black.

TILT MY CROWN TO THE STREETS
Johnazia Gray & *Danielle Offett*

CHAPTER TWELVE
DERRIA

I enjoyed spending the day with my sister, Ms. Shirley, and my niece before me and Semaj left to head out to Miami tomorrow. I had never been and I was dying to get a taste of the food, the beach, and all the fun Semaj had told me we were bound to have. Being engaged to my man was the best feeling ever. He treated me like a queen and I had absolutely no worries. The condo he had just purchased for us downtown was beautiful and that was where we spent most of our time. We spent so much time together that our folks were feeling some type of way from staying away from them for days.

I really wanted Dola and Chazae to join us but they had their own thing going on which wasn't a problem. Times like this, I wished Ashlee had a boyfriend.

"Titi, will I be the flower girl at your wedding?" Princess asked me.

"Of course you'll be my flower girl, baby." I kissed her cheek.

She smiled and nodded her head. We sat in the living room on Dola's sectional sofa and watched the movie *Hidden Figures* on the Fire Stick. It was a very good movie.

"I'm just so happy for y'all, Derria," Ms. Shirley said. "I tell you one thing, if I was a little younger, I'd propose to that daddy of theirs."

We all laughed.

"Say what, ma?" Dola asked her.

"Y'all heard me. That man would make me do the dummy how these young girls doing. Dumb asses get on their knees asking a man for his hand in marriage." She shook her head. "That's what I'd do for Mr. Dom though."

Dola was too tickled.

Mr. Dom was a very handsome and nice man. I always enjoyed being around him because he always treated me like I was family. He was very respectful to women, one of the reasons my man was so blessed in that area. Mr. Dom and I had our very own relationship outside of Semaj that I loved and appreciated. He was a cool dude.

I hadn't talked to Semaj since he had left earlier this morning, and I knew he was doing something he had no business because it wasn't like him not to text me or call me back. I knew he'd probably use me spending time with my family as an excuse to not responding to me, but I was going to get his sneaky ass for sure. I had no doubt in my mind that he was dealing with Tauris and those drugs, and it was beginning to piss me off that he was still involved with the shit when I specifically told him how I felt about it. I tried so hard not to step over his toes and talk to his father, but that was what he was going to make me do. Semaj knew absolutely nothing about the streets. He was a pretty boy and I loved that. I didn't want a nigga who was in the streets. Hell, if that was the case I would've been in a relationship long before he came into my life. He was perfect for me just how he was and I stressed that to him daily.

"Hey, Ashlee is going to stop by and bring me something," I told Dola.

She rolled her eyes. "I hear you."

"Why you do that all the time?" I asked her.

Johnazia Gray & *Danielle Offett*

Every time I mentioned Ashlee's name, she would trip. My girl wasn't that bad.

"That's not your friend, Derria. It doesn't take a blind man to see that girl is jealous of you. Tell her, Ma." She looked at Shirley.

"Well, Derria know I can't stand the heifer. She know that girl ain't for her."

I waved them off. Just when I was getting up to go to the bathroom, there was a loud knock at the door. We were in the projects and crackheads and children were always beating down people's doors for different reasons, so I thought nothing of it. I turned around and peeked my head around the corner.

"Stop knocking on my door like your ass have no sense! I'm coming!" Dola snapped to whoever it was.

When Dola opened the door, two men carried Chazae in and he was covered in blood, sweat, and tears, literally.

"Oh my God, what happened, Chazae?" Dola screamed.

Princess began to cry when she saw Chazae crying.

"Oh my God. Come on, Princess, let's go upstairs to my apartment," Ms. Shirley said, covering Princess' eyes from the messy scene.

"My brother," Chazae cried.

My heart raced. "Where's Semaj, Chazae?" I panicked.

"Answer her, Chazae. Where's Semaj?" Dola shook him.

The two men that brought him in looked sad. When I looked at them for answers, they dropped their heads.

"Chazae, please, tell me where Semaj is." Tears spilled down my cheeks.

"He's dead, Derria." He cried harder.

Johnazia Gray & *Danielle Offett*

"*Noooooooooooooooo!*" I ran toward him, slapped him, and pulled on his jacket. "*Noooooooooooooooooo!* Where is Semaj?"

"Derria!" Dola tried to console me but she only ended up getting slapped, and getting her hair pulled.

"Get off of me!" I kicked and screamed. "Where is Semaj?"

The men separated me from my sister. "Calm down, ma," one of them told me.

"Titi!" Princess cried for me.

"Take her upstairs, Ms. Shirley, please," Dola begged her. She nodded and grabbed her hand.

There was no way he could be dead. No way. I had just seen him that morning. He had been perfectly fine before we parted ways.

"Chazae, what happened?" Dola cried and asked.

"We had a shootout with some niggas at a trap and he was there. *He was there.* He wasn't supposed to fucking be there."

I screamed and fell on the floor. I'd continuously told him that it could've come to this, and he'd promised me that he wasn't going to involve himself. Not only that, but he'd assured me that he was going to be okay. Now, he was gone. He was dead. He was my heart. The reason I was so happy in my life. He was my everything besides my sister. He completed me.

"Where's your father?" Dola asked him.

"The feds came and picked him up not too long ago."

"Where's Semaj?" I asked.

"He's fucking dead, Derria. He's dead," Chazae yelled.

"Where's his body? I need to see him. Take me to the hospital so I can go see him. He's not dead." I shook my head with tears spilling down my face. I refused to believe that my baby was gone.

"We had to leave him," one of the men said.

"What!" I tried to attack Chazae again.

"Derria, please calm down, sis. Please." Dola tried hugging me but I snatched away from her. I grabbed my car keys and ran out the door. I saw Ashlee pulling up but I didn't give a fuck about her at the time.

"Derria!" Dola called after me.

I ignored her as I got into my car. Everyone was standing outside of their apartments staring at us as if we were crazy.

I got in my car and drove. I didn't care where I was going, I just had to get the fuck away from them. I had to go and find Semaj. I ran straight through a red light and didn't even see the truck that crashed into me from the side. I closed my eyes tight as the car flipped over what felt like five times. When it stopped, I knew the car was upside down. I could feel blood gushing from my head and into my eyes, blocking my vision. I thought I smelled gas and some fire, but I blacked out seconds later.

CHAPTER THIRTEEN
DOM

I sat in this cold ass interrogation room and I already knew what time it was. The entire time I was here, I could only think of my son, Chazae, and how he'd begged me not to fuck with that cat, Odney. It was crazy, but I'd felt this shit coming soon. Something about life had felt off lately and it was like that ever since I had allowed that nigga to start supplying dope to my camp. They had enough information to put me away for a long time but I still wasn't saying shit until my lawyers came—I knew they could help me. If not get me all the way off, I knew that they could cut a nigga some slack. My only reason of living was for my boys, honestly, and because I had raised two men I really didn't have shit to worry about. I believed in God, and I knew how this shit went. You live by the sword and you die by the sword. I guess it was just my time. The only part of happiness I felt right now was that I had a smart ass son who knew better than I did. I had taught Chazae well and because he knew that Odney nigga was out to get me before I did, I knew he could run this empire without me leading him. I didn't have to worry about him anymore. He was smart as hell when it came to this shit. I had a son who was smart in the streets and the books, and I had a book smart son. That was enough for me. Semaj didn't need to know the ropes of the streets because he had too much of his mom's genes in him. He was a little too weak for the streets and that was okay. As long as he knew something.

My two lawyers walked into the room and I couldn't have been happier. I was honestly just ready to call my sons and let

Johnazia Gray & Danielle Offett

them know that I was good, and to be taken to a cell so I could get the fuck out of this creepy, spooky ass room.

"I'm glad y'all here, man," I told them.

I knew they were looking sad because they probably thought that it was nothing they could do for me, and that was okay. I mean, if they couldn't do anything to help, I could always get Chazae to get me some better lawyers. One thing about being in the dope game was money ruled everything, and the money that I had would definitely get one of these lawyers around here to make some shit happen for me. I was a patient nigga and I had been my entire life, so laying down while they did the work was nothing to me.

The two detectives walked in but nobody was saying anything.

"Speak. What the fuck is wrong with y'all?" I asked my lawyers.

"Dom, man," Mr. Sanchez said to me. He and his son was big time lawyers that had been working for me for years.

"Dom, what?" I asked.

The two detectives begin to giggle.

"It's Semaj, man," Sanchez said to me.

The look in his eyes when he said my son's name said everything.

"What about Semaj? Where he at?"

"Semaj was killed, man. He was shot today."

When he finished his sentence, my head began to spin and everything in the room was multiplied. I blinked repeatedly and tried holding on to the table because it felt like I was about to fall backwards. When I heard the detectives giggling, I snapped out of my trance and hopped over the table. I attacked both of them at the same time and tried my best to kill them. The nerve of those disrespectful ass pigs to laugh at some shit like that. I grabbed the black one and tried to poke his eyes out with my fingers while I grabbed the other one and smashed his head into the concrete wall. His loud screams were satisfying. Once he was down on the ground, I tried choking the other out. I almost succeeded until my lawyers tried so hard to get me off of them. I was fucking them up.

"Dom, chill out, man. Stop it right now!" Sanchez tackled me. By that time, SWAT officers came in ready to beat the shit out of me. I was beaten with the sticks but I felt nothing. I felt numb as they restrained me and handcuffed me.

"Not my baby boy, man!" I screamed and cried as the officers dragged me out. "My son!"

Suddenly, my stomach turned and I threw up everywhere. I didn't even get a chance to figure out what happened. Semaj couldn't be dead. How could Semaj be dead? How could I handle shit myself while being locked up? I felt dehydrated and it felt like I was about to faint.

"I need to see a doctor or something," I told the officers right before they slung me into the box and left me as if the worst news of my life hadn't just been told to me. I slid down the wall and cried like a baby just before blacking out.

*****

It was the third day that I had been in the box, and I didn't know whether I was going or coming. My lawyers had worked hard enough for me to get a few visits a week, but I wasn't interested in any. The detectives that I had attacked pressed charges on me which only made things worse for me, but I didn't give a fuck. Chazae had come up here two days straight and I refused to see him. I couldn't face him and not be able to see Semaj. Every day, I lay on the floor and stared at the ceiling. Whenever they gave me food, I threw it in the trash. I had no appetite and I had no desire to do anything. I knew I had lost a few pounds from the stress and not eating. Hell, I didn't even want anything to drink. If I could've lain there and died; that would've been okay with me. When my lawyers came to visit me, I was forced to see them but I made it clear that I didn't want to hear anything about my son's death. I was still debating if I wanted to attend the funereal because I knew I wasn't strong enough for it. Because I knew that Chazae was handling Semaj's funeral arrangements, I had no worries. I honestly didn't even know the full story as to why Semaj had been murdered, and the mindset that I was in, I wasn't going to get revenge until I bounced back. Every day I cried myself to sleep. That was actually the only way I could sleep. Nobody understood how much my sons meant to me. They were my life and I did everything for them. Those were my boys and they had been with me since birth. When Charae left me, I had to play both parts and that made me and my sons closer. To not have one was going to be hard to adjust to. Whoever fucking said I had to adjust to it anyways?

My door opened and two guards that my lawyers added to payroll stood over me.

"You got an important visit, man," Officer Troy said.

I put my hands over my eyes. "Tell whoever it is I don't want to see nobody, man. What y'all niggas getting paid for?" I frowned.

"Sanchez said that if Charae came, to make you come out this room. So get the fuck up, man. You're going to kill yourself just laying here," he said.

TILT MY CROWN TO THE STREETS
Johnazia Gray & Danielle Offett

Hearing Charae's name made my heart race like a bitch. I didn't know why she was here to see me, but I would be a lying old ass nigga if I said that it didn't bring a little happiness to my broken heart. I still loved that woman and I'd do anything to have her back. I didn't give a fuck that she was an attorney. Charae had been loyal to me before I pushed her to those drugs, and every day of my life I regretted that shit. I had been so focused on the streets back then that I made my woman feel useless, worthless, and I was unappreciative of her love. They weren't lying when they said you don't miss them until they're gone because when Charae left me and got on drugs, I was sick. I tried my best to get her some help but she didn't want it. When she got clean on her own and moved on with her life, I gave up on love completely. If it wasn't her, then I didn't want anyone. Chazae and his mother had the same fucking attitude which was the reason they couldn't get along with each other. I hated the fact that my boy was so stern when it came to not wanting to deal with her, but Chazae was a hard nut to crack. Stubborn as fuck is what most people would call it. For years, I chased behind Charae and tried to get her back but she acted as if she just wasn't interested anymore. I knew it was because she was the law and I was still the king of these streets, but if she would've taken me back, I probably would've retired.

I got up and threw some water over my face before I let them put the cuffs on my wrists and around my ankles. I hated feeling like I was a fucking animal locked up in a cage, but that was what it was, I guess. Only because I was seeing Charae I wish I would've looked halfway decent, but then again, I didn't care. She'd seen me at my worst before.

Instead of going to the visitation area, we were walking to one of the interrogation rooms and my blood began to boil. *Is this bitch coming to question me about drugs when my son was dead?* I thought to myself.

"No worries, boss man. This room has no cameras and no one is listening to y'all," Troy told me.

I guess he noticed the look on my face.

"Thirty minutes to an hour. We'll be standing out here waiting on you," Tony told me.

I nodded, walked into the room, and there she was—the beautiful woman that had stolen my heart when I was only nineteen years old. Looking at Charae, you would never be able to tell that she'd had a past of being on drugs. She was absolutely gorgeous and her beautiful, big round, brown eyes were glistening. She had picked up some weight since the last time I had seen her out in public, but she looked good. Her style was always on point so I wasn't surprised that she looked so stunning. I took a seat across from her and stared a hole through her. This was the woman that I remembered falling in love with. The room was so silent I could hear pins drop. When I looked down at her hand and saw the wedding ring I had given her back then, I almost choked up. It wasn't on her ring finger but she still wore it. I wasn't sure if she had put it on to make me happy since I was going through so much, but if she did she'd succeeded.

She cleared her throat. "How are you holding up, Dom?"

"I'm not. How about you?" I asked her.

"You know Semaj was like a son to me, so I'm just as heartbroken as everyone else. I'm not sure if y'all knew it or not, but Semaj and I still were communicating and hanging out together." Her eyes watered. When a tear slid down her cheek, I couldn't hold back my tears. Just that fast, the pain resurfaced.

"My own son wants nothing to do with me, but Semaj accepted me and understood. God, I loved that boy." She broke down.

I put my head down and shook it. All of this was my fault.

"I'm sorry." I looked into her hurt eyes.

"I tried reaching out to Chazae but he wants nothing to do with me. He's so mean." She chuckled through her tears. "I wanted to help him with the funeral arrangements but I guess he doesn't want that." She shrugged.

"I'll holler at him about that," I assured her. "You look good," I tried changing the subject.

"Thank you. You look good too despite your roughness." She smiled.

"I'ma be all right." I shook my head.

"I know you're coming home for the funeral."

"I don't know if I am or not. I honestly don't even want to believe that Semaj is gone and I don't want to talk about it."

"I understand." She dropped her head.

"I see you're still wearing the ring."

She began to play around with it. "I never took it off. Just switched the finger."

"Lets me know you still love me." I chuckled, "You know when Semaj proposed to Derria, I went and had a ring made exactly like that so he could propose to her with it and he loved it man. She did too." I wiped the tears that threatened to fall from my eyes. "We raised that little nigga right, man. He was the pretty boy version of me." I burst into tears. "I wasn't there to protect my son. When he needed me the most, I wasn't there for him." I dropped my head and sobbed.

"Hey," she walked over to me and rubbed my back, "it's not your fault, Dom. Don't blame yourself for this."

Johnazia Gray & Danielle Offett

"It is my fault. If I would've paid more attention to Semaj, I would've known something was going on with him."

When I calmed down, she walked back to her side of the table and sat down. When she pulled out the notepad and pen, I looked at her and frowned.

"I can get you out of here where you can get home to some peace and sanity if you work with me, Dom. All I need you to do is take out the man who took you down."

"Are you fucking serious right now, Charae? My son is dead and you want me to fucking snitch? What the fuck kind of nigga you think I am?"

"You don't need to be in this place while you're going through this. I can help you, but only if you help me, help you."

"Let me ask you a question, Charae. Have I ever been a snitch?"

She shook her head.

"So what makes you think I'ma start?"

"He fucking snitched on you and it's not about you, Dom. Chazae is about to turn these streets upside fucking down and if you don't get out and tame him, he's going to be right here with you. Look at this shit!" She slammed a file on the table and fingered through it. It was pictures of Chazae making transactions with some of his workers and some more shit.

"My son's name hit my desk yesterday. I'm not here for me. It's plenty niggas in New Orleans I can take down besides y'all."

I shook my head.

"I'm not telling on nobody, Charae. I will talk to Chazae and let him know to slow his roll but I don't have it in me to snitch. I'm sorry, ma." I leaned over and kissed her cheek and turned to walk away. I took one final look at her and it broke my heart to see her crying like that, but I couldn't do it. Chazae was a smart nigga. All I had to do was warn him and he would slow down, but as far as me telling I would rot in my cell before I did that. It was a lot of things I played about but snitching was not one of them. I was a real street nigga and some shit you just couldn't do. I had something out for that Odney nigga and when I got done with him, he was going to wish he never ran his fucking mouth to the pigs.

"I love you, Charae. Take care," I said before I hit the door for the guards to let me out.

*****

I pulled up to the Franklin Avenue Baptist Church in the jail van and the church was packed. My son was truly loved, man. I felt like shit that I had to come to the funeral dressed in a jail uniform, but I couldn't change that shit. When they opened the door for me to get out, it felt like my chest tightened up. I was hooked up with a nice haircut so that made me look a little decent. I got out of the van and all eyes, cellphones, and cameras were on me. The people couldn't even respect the fact that I was grieving over my dead son. They just wanted some shit to post on social media. Life was crazy.

Chazae was pissed off with me when I reached out to him about me and his mama's visit. The little nigga was in his feelings about me turning down his visits and not Charae's. I somewhat understood though. I neglected him when he needed me the most, but he didn't understand that I didn't want to face one son and not the other. Nobody would probably be able to understand that. He stood his ground and didn't let Charae have any parts of Semaj's funeral arrangements and I found that to be fucked up.

He was being nasty and heartless and I didn't raise him like that. It went from me refusing his visits to him refusing to talk to me. From what I heard, he had shut the world out besides his girlfriend, Dola. I had to talk to her soon to get more information on what was really going through his mind.

The officers pushed me through the crowd and I walked in the church. When I saw my boy lying in the casket, I wanted to run out of the church and back into the van, but I had to be strong. He looked so handsome and Chazae had laid him away just right. I leaned over and kissed his hard face. Who would've ever fucking thought that I would be burying Semaj? My goofy child, my sweet child, my school boy?

I turned and faced Chazae who had murder written across his face. He looked like he hated me, but it wasn't the time for that. I needed love and he did too. I wasn't even aware that Derria was in a wheelchair with a cast on her arm and her foot in a boot. She sat in her chair in a corner with her head down. I shook my head and took a seat by Chazae.

"Charae's over there, nigga. Go be with that bitch. It's obvious that you wanted her by your side more than you wanted me. I'm the one who's broken, nigga! You was supposed to be my best friend besides my brother, nigga. You turned on me for that bitch. But she's only using you so she can win a case in court," he whispered in my ear and got up. When he went to the other side to sit with Dola, a tear slid down my face. My son hated me. The little nigga hated me.

The preacher preached and the choir sang. The cries and screams in the church made me weak. I continuously stared at Chazae but he wouldn't even look at me. He cried in Derria's arms like a baby and he wouldn't even come to me. We needed each other.

The family gathered around Semaj's casket and took a final look before they closed it and the loud scream that escaped Derria's mouth made me fall down to my knees.

"Get up, baby. Pleaseeeeeee Semaj, get up!" She kicked, cried, and screamed. "Please, Semaj, our wedding is next year, one month after our graduation, don't leave me like this." The ushers rushed over to console her but she was kicking and screaming. Almost falling out of her wheelchair, Dola rolled her out. You could hear her screams until she was completely out of the church.

"I'ma handle this, son. I promise," I cried and kissed Semaj.

I took one final look at Chazae who was clearly broken and shook my head. I didn't know what to do or what to say. Shit was fucked up.

I looked at the officers and motioned for them to take me back to the jail.

That was a day I'd never forget.

CHAPTER FOURTEEN

TAURIS

As I vacuumed the white substance into my nose, my nostrils began to burn and my pupils dilated. Once the numbness overcame my body, I sat the plate of pure cocaine in my lap and rested my head against the headboard. This was some good ass shit we were selling. I knew this was against everything we stood for. We always went by the "never use the shit you sell" motto, but I was fucked up. This white girl was the only shit to numb my pain and keep me somewhat sane.

I had taken a small business trip to Texas and next thing I knew, I got a million and seven texts and voicemails telling me that Semaj was dead. A nigga was really fucked up over that shit. Just because me and Chazae were on bad terms didn't mean I was on some grimy shit with Semaj. I really considered that nigga my brother. When Dom and Chazae treated me like a bald-headed step child, he was always keeping it one hundred with me. The fucked up part about it was, I couldn't even attend my brother's funeral because of Chazae's bitch ass! He was gon' end up making me body his ass! That nigga really had niggas out looking for me. Not just any niggas, *my* niggas! The same niggas *I* put on payroll! Where the fuck was the loyalty? So, I had no choice but to be hiding in this fucking rat infested motel until I came up with a way to handle this shit.

"Damn, is you gone be stingy with the plate all night? I'm trying to get right too," a squeaky female voice snapped.

With glazed over eyes, I looked over at the naked bitch sitting next to me. I forgot she was even here until she started

138

yelling in my ear with her annoying ass voice. I met Cashmere at the strip club and we'd been kicking it ever since. Standing at five two, she was still a brick house and put all them other bitches to shame. That was until she opened her mouth and wouldn't shut up.

"Hello," she sang. "You gone pass the plate of white or what? You New Orleans niggas are stingy as fuck. That's exactly why I don't fuck with y'all broke asses. I should've left the club with Juwan's fine ass. Now *that* is a boss ass nigga. He got the streets on lock *and* he ain't selfish with his shit."

Who the fuck was she talking to? Did she not know I who I was? Fuck that nigga, Juwan! I was about to take over Texas too and leave his ass begging to be on my payroll. That was the problem with these bitches. They didn't respect my hustle but this bitch was about to learn a valuable lesson.

Knocking the plate of cocaine onto the floor, I reached over and put my hand around her neck, cutting of her oxygen supply. She kicked her legs frantically as I yanked her body up the headboard and slammed her into the wall. I was now standing up on the bed and watching her struggle to breathe.

"Please," she whispered, clawing at my hand.

"Please what?" I asked. "Please what, Cash? Disrespect me like that again and I'll kill you with my bare hands. Ya hear me? I'm the muthafuckin king of these streets not that whack ass nigga Juwan!" I yelled, spit flying in her face. "Ya hear me?"

She attempted to nod her head but could barely move. I loosened my grip so she could respond to me.

"Who's the king of these streets?"

"You...you are," she said, trying to breathe through her mouth.

Satisfied with her answer, I released my grip and allowed her body to collapse onto the bed. She immediately balled up and tried to get back her breathing pattern that she had been deprived of a few seconds ago. I didn't know if it was the cocaine or the fact she named me the king of the streets, but it made my dick hard and now she was going to get some of this king dick.

"Bitch, turn over and stop crying," I commanded.

As if she didn't hear me, she lay there crying her eyes out.

"What are you crying for, ma? You said you like it rough," I joked while turning her over by her legs. She tried to clamp them together, but I pried them open and positioned myself in between. She might've hated me right now but by the way that pussy was glistening, I knew it loved me.

Taking my nine-inch erect penis, I rubbed it in her wetness like I was playing in a puddle on a rainy day.

"So you gone rape me, Tee?" Cashmere cried.

"What?"

I stopped completely and looked at her like she was crazy. Rape? All I could think about was on *Baby Boy* when Rodney tried to get him some welcome home pussy, and Yvette hit him with "you gone rape me in front of my son?" I pulled up my sweat pants with a quickness. I was a lot of things but rapist wasn't one of them. I was a good-looking nigga and could get any pussy I wanted, including hers just a few minutes ago. My high was fully blown. I had ninety-nine problems and raping her wasn't going to be one of them.

"Bitch, we been fucking for two weeks straight and now that shit gets a little rough, you want to call out rape? It was okay when yo' freaky ass was asking me to choke you and pull yo' hair but now it's rape?"

Johnazia Gray & Danielle Offett

I picked up the few scraps of clothing she came with and threw them at her. "Bitch get the fuck out," I snapped.

She scrambled off the bed and slid into a skin-tight dress that had rips in it. There was even a rip in the breast area exposing her nipples but she had the nerve to call out rape. As she opened the door to leave, she looked at me with hatred.

"You're gonna regret putting your hands on me."

"And you're gonna regret not sucking this dick before you leave. Now get the fuck out."

She left, slamming the door and causing the cheap wall decorations to fall off.

My business in Texas was over and I was done hiding from Chazae. He had niggas looking for me so I would save him the trouble and go to him. My original plan was for me and Lance to take his crown and I still planned to. Sorry, baby brother, but "one dead monkey don't stop no show."

*****

It took nine hours to get back to my hood but I wasted no time before I started making moves. I made a few stops through the hood just to get my face out there. Some niggas were genuinely happy to see me while others gave me the side eye and pulled out their phones. I already knew they were hitting up Chazae, being a bunch of do boys, but that was exactly what I wanted. He wasn't on the block yet but I would definitely be seeing him soon.

First, I had to make a stop to see my cousin, Lance. I needed a few answers and to get some shit straight. Even though he didn't pull the trigger, he shouldn't have sent Semaj on a run knowing Chazae was gunning for him. It was partially his fault my brother was gone.

Lance had already been out and about and asked me to meet him at some spot on Religious Street. The GPS pulled me into the parking lot of *The Monkey Room*. I spotted him already leaning up against his car. Parking next to him, I got out, looked around the area, and dapped him up.

"What up, Dope?"

"Nothing major, out here moving with much needed pressure in these streets. How was the trip?" he asked, sparking up a blunt.

"It was cool. So, what happened?" I wanted to get straight to the point. I had already heard the story a million times, but I needed him to tell me why he went against my orders.

He shrugged his shoulders. "I didn't kill the little nigga."

"I didn't say you did. What I want to know is why you sent him out there without my permission. I told you to keep tabs on him in the meetings, not send him on runs. He was working for *me*, not you."

I didn't even notice how pissed I was until my jaws began to clench.

"Look, *cuzzo*, don't poke ya chest out at me because the little nigga got some hot shit in him. He wanted to be about his dope boy life, he needed to put in work, just like the rest of us. Let's not forget, you brought me down here to help take over. I'll let it slide this time but you and I both know, I don't take orders from no nigga so you might want to come at me a li'l different. You think you're the only one who took a loss? I'm pissed some of the niggas are gone too. At first, it was just business but now it's personal. Trust me, that nigga Chazae will be doing more than releasing his crown and that's on my kids."

Johnazia Gray & *Danielle* Offett

The plan was never to kill Chazae. It was just to rid him of his crown, make me the king, and have my cousin as my right hand man but by the look in Lance's eyes, I knew it was a different plan now. Lance wanted blood. I had expected there to be bloodshed but not blood of someone close to home. Shit was about to get real.

"Aye, I'ma holla at you though. I'm here with my kid and baby moms."

I was wondering why this nigga asked to meet at a kids' land.

Looking up, I saw a chick holding hands with a little girl walking in our direction. The girl looked familiar, but I couldn't put my finger on it.

"Here they go right now," he said, looking in the same direction. "Dola, babe, hurry up!"

"I'm not your damn, babe, Lance. I told you that," she snapped.

Dola! I had heard that name before and immediately panicked when her eyes met mine. Shit! I readjusted my baseball cap, hoping to shield my identity.

"Damn, you didn't tell me that was your baby moms. Meet me at the spot tonight at eleven. Fuck!" I whispered to him in a hushed tone.

I didn't even wait for his response before jumping back in my car and speeding off. I could see both Lance and Dola eyeing my ride as I sped out the parking lot. My windows were tinted, but I didn't want to take a chance of her trying to get a better look at me. We never chilled but I knew Chazae was fucking with a stripper bitch named Dola. There weren't too many Dola's but I prayed this one wasn't her. If it was, this could really put some dents in our plans.

Johnazia Gray & Danielle Offett

My phone lit up and I opened the text.

Chazae: You a bold nigga walking the streets like I wouldn't find out. Ain't no beef unless I find out you on some other shit. Meet me tomorrow at nine.

Damn, word traveled fast. It really pissed me off that this nigga was always two steps ahead of me but it was cool. Now I just needed to talk to Lance and get that bitch Dola on our team. Then I would have the upper hand again and his bitch ass won't see it coming.

CHAPTER FIFTEEN

DOLA

I was extremely frustrated that Lance had invited himself into my crib. All he was supposed to do was drop us off and keep it moving. Of course, he promised Princess to have a tea party and she damn near dragged him inside. He knew damn well he didn't want to do a tea party. He just wanted to be around me. While they were in her room playing, I went to the kitchen and fixed myself a glass of wine.

Even though I didn't want him there, it was bothering me even more because the wheels in my head were turning. I'd never formally met Tauris but I had seen his picture when he called Chazae a few times. He tried to pull his hat down but I knew it was him. He was acting real suspicious and looked at me like he had seen a ghost. What business did he have with Lance? Was Lance coming really for our daughter or was he still up to the same hood shit?

"Fuck it, let me find out what this nigga is really up to," I said, jumping off the couch and heading to Princess' room.

As I approached the door, I heard muffled sounds. I looked through the cracked door and saw Lance looking out the window, whispering into the phone. He wasn't too good at whispering because I could still hear him.

"Look, when you find that bitch ass nigga, Chazae, don't touch a hair on his head. Bring him to me so I can be the one to put a bullet in him. He wants war then he got it. Tauris might want to pacify him but you know that's not how I get down. It's murder time."

The caller said something causing him to laugh.

"Yeah, I'm meeting with Tauris today. Cousin or not, he better be ready to get his hands dirty or I won't mind knocking him off too. Aight, I'll hit you up after I meet with him."

I didn't realize I wasn't breathing until I began to feel light headed. I bumped into the wall as I tried to backpedal away from the door.

"You straight?"

I looked up to see Lance eyeing me curiously. I didn't even see him open the door.

"I-I, yeah, I'm good. Just was coming to check on y'all. Should've turned the hallway light on and I wouldn't have ran into the wall."

He stared at me before chuckling. "Yo' ass always been clumsy. I really came over here to talk about us but I got to make some runs. Can I come back over once Princess is sleep to talk? I know you say you're done with a nigga but—"

I cut him off. "Sure. Just text me when you're on your way."

He looked shocked that I wasn't fighting him on this. Little did he know, I didn't plan on being home when he got back. I just needed to get rid of him so I could go warn Chazae. I couldn't believe his own best friend was turning on him. I didn't know if I was a pawn in Lance's game or not, so I had to keep an eye on him.

He kissed Princess and made his way to the door. Once outside, I watched from the window until I saw his car exit the neighborhood altogether. Once he was out of sight, I threw on my jacket and shoes and went to Princess' room to grab her. Thankfully, she still had her shoes on.

"Come on, baby. I need you to go to Mama Shirley's house for tonight."

"Are you going to work tonight?" she asked, helping me put her jacket on.

"No, but I have grown up things to take care of so come on, little girl."

Exiting my apartment, I looked both ways before making a beeline to Ms. Shirley's. You would've thought I was running from my pimp the way I was banging her door down.

Johnazia Gray & Danielle Offett

"Chile, what in the hell is wrong with you? Why didn't you use your damn key?" she asked, holding her oversized robe together.

"I'm sorry, Mama. I wasn't thinking. Is it okay if Princess stays the night?"

Not waiting for an invitation, Princess slid inside and ran to her room.

"Is everything all right?" I could read the worry in her eyes.

Lying wasn't my thing, but I didn't feel like telling her what was on my mind just yet. Self-consciously, I ran my fingers through my hair.

"I'm fine. I just need to go see Chazae for a minute."

The mention of his name caused a smile to form. "I knew you would get tired of using those toys and get you some real d–"

I put my hand up. "Ewwww. I am not having that conversation with you. I'll be back in the morning."

As I walked down the stairs, I heard her still talking. "Yo' ass better bring me back a pack of Newports!"

She knew damn well I wasn't bringing her back those cancer sticks.

Getting in the car, I called Chazae and let him know I was on my way. I honestly thought our souls were connected because he could sense something was wrong with me by just hearing my voice. The shit I just heard wasn't something to just tell over the phone. I needed to get to him before Tauris snake ass did.

*****

"How you holding up?" I asked, taking a seat next to him on the couch.

"I'm straight. Just making moves and laying low."

By the looks of him, he wasn't straight. The man sitting next to me was unkempt and scruffy. He had let his curly locks run wild over his head and his beard had grown out. Don't get me wrong, he was still looking good enough to eat but this wasn't him. I could look into his eyes and tell that a piece of him was missing. His eyes were much colder and I didn't know how to console him.

I watched him as he threw back shot after shot, not even stopping when his throat started to burn. It hurt for me to see him like this. I took the bottle off the table and went to the kitchen to pour it out. I knew he was hurting, but he wasn't going to drink himself to death on my watch. I returned and took a seat next to him like nothing happened.

"You know Semaj planned on opening up his own chain of hotels? That nigga was smart as fuck and had big goals. He wouldn't even let me help fund it with his stubborn ass."

We both let out an uncomfortable chuckle.

"Yeah, my little nigga was supposed to be a legit businessman. He was supposed to make me and Pops proud and do better than us. That's all I wanted was for him to be better than me." I could see the tears threatening to escape his eyelids. "But I killed him. I killed my own fucking brother."

"Don't you even fix your mouth to say that. You didn't kill him. He was at the wrong place at the wrong time. Semaj knew he shouldn't have been out there. He even told Derria he had a bad feeling about doing that last run. I know that nothing I can say will take away the pain, but what you won't do is feel guilty about something you had no control over."

"Yeah, well until I body the niggas I was gunning for, I'm holding myself responsible. The least I can do is get the niggas who had my brother out there doing runs like he wasn't a fucking boss. I let every muthafucka know that Semaj was off limits. So, who had the balls to put him on to some corner boy shit? I won't sleep, eat, or stop painting the city red until I get my hands on them niggas."

The look in his eyes was of pure rage. Looking into them was like looking into the eyes of the devil. It scared the shit out of me and made me second guess telling him what I knew. If I told him, more people were going to die but if I didn't tell him, people were still going

Johnazia Gray & *Danielle Offett*

to die. At least, if I told him, he would be able to sleep at night without watching over his shoulder for that snake he had around him.

I took a deep breath. "Zae, I need to tell you something."

His eyes softened. "Damn, Ma. I'm tripping. Wassup? I know you sounded down over the phone. You good?"

I nodded my head. "I need to tell you something. It's about Semaj."

"What about my bro?"

I took another deep breath and filled him in on my relations with Lance and what I heard him saying a minute ago. His face was emotionless when I told him about me seeing him meet up with Tauris. As a matter of fact, he just gave me a blank stare as I told him everything.

"So, Dope is Lance and Lance is your baby daddy?" he repeated.

I nodded my head. "Tauris is Lance's cousin and I think, no I *know* they're trying to set you up. I don't know what they have planned but I heard your name come up."

He sat back on the couch and looked straight ahead. I knew it was a lot for him to digest. His own friend was against him and could be the reason his brother was dead. I moved closer to him only to be met by the barrel of his gun. Instantly, I froze. What the fuck was going on?

"Bitch, you think you can play me?" He grabbed a handful of my hair and placed the gun directly under my chin. "This whole time, I thought you was really about to ride for a nigga but you were plotting on me all along," he spat, lips tightening.

"Wh-wh-what are you talking about, Zae? I just told you what went down. I would never try to play you."

"So this same nigga that's been trying to take over my shit just so happens to be your baby daddy? You must think I'm the dumbest nigga on the planet?"

The entire ride over, I thought of a way to tell him everything. Not once did I think it would backfire on me and that I would end up looking into the eyes of death.

"So what was the plan? You were gonna make me fall for yo' hoe ass then set me up for yo' man to kill me? What, you was fucking Tauris too?"

Fucking Tauris? Where did that come from?

"Zae, just let me try to explain better," I begged.

"Shut the fuck up!" He snatched my head back and pressed the gun harder into my chin. "Bitches like you is why I don't trust you hoes. The only reason you're still breathing is because Derria still holds a piece of my brother." He let go of my hair and lowered his gun. "Get the fuck out. Let that nigga of yours know that his brains belong to me."

"But–"

"I don't want to hear that shit you're talking. Get the fuck out before I change my mind and put a bullet in you."

I wanted to protest and beg for him to listen to me, but the look in his eyes and the way he was still gripping his gun made me stay quiet. I pleaded with my eyes as I walked to the door.

"Dola."

I turned around with a half-smile. He came back to his senses faster than I thought. I knew he didn't actually believe I would set him up.

"You're dead to me. Next time I see you, there will be a bullet with your name on it."

Those words hit me like a ton of bricks. I couldn't help the tears from falling as I ran to my car. How did we get here? We were finally establishing something and letting down walls. Now, he wanted to kill me. I pulled off, going to the only person who could feel my pain: my sister. I knew she was hurting but we could hurt together.

*****

Tilt My Crown To The Streets
Johnazia Gray & Danielle Offett

"Sissy!" I cried, running into Derria's apartment. I knew she was depressed because there were empty bottles of liquor and cigarettes everywhere. I never saw her smoke a cigarette a day in her life. Seeing her place like this made me wipe my tears and put on my big sister panties. She needed me far more than I needed her to mend my heart.

"Derria!" I yelled, walking down the hall leading to her bedroom. I looked around and it looked just as bad as the living room, if not worse. Something on the dresser caught my eye. I walked up to get a closer look and almost lost my damn mind. Breaking my thoughts, I heard a sound coming from the bathroom. I picked up the mirror that held the white lines of coke and stormed into the direction of the bathroom.

"Derria, I'm gonna kick your little ass! What the fuck—"

My words were cut off by the sight in front of me. Derria was slumped over with her head dangling over the tub. Blood trickled down from where she had just hit her head. Next to her laid a rolled-up dollar bill and powder had spilled out onto the floor. I couldn't believe that I had caught her doing drugs! I dropped the glass and ran toward her.

"Come on, baby girl. Get up," I cried, smacking her face repeatedly. She was unresponsive.

I ran back into the room, grabbed her phone, and ran back to her side.

"You can't do this to me, Sissy. I need you," I cried.

"9-1-1, what's your emergency?"

"My sister, she's not moving. I think she overdosed. Please send someone to help her!"

"Are you able to provide an address?"

I rambled off the address and anything else I knew.

"Just please send somebody. She's not moving," I screamed, still smacking her face, hoping to get a response.

"Try to remain calm, ma'am. Help is on the way."

Help is on the way? I didn't need help on the way. I needed help to come save my sister *now*. I pulled her body into my arms and rocked back and forth as my tears fell into her tangled hair. When did

151

she start doing drugs? How did I miss this? Was I too busy with my own shit to notice she needed me?

"Please, sissy. Please don't leave me. You can't leave me. You can't leave Princess. You hear me?" I cried, wiping my tears off her face. "It's us against the world, right?"

I heard the front door flying open followed by the paramedics rushing into the bathroom. They pried her out of my arms and began to check for a pulse. God knew she was my everything. He wouldn't take her away from me. I had lived my whole life for her and without her, I would probably die. I looked on in fear as they performed CPR.

Lord please save her for me, I prayed.

"We have a pulse!" I heard them yell.

CHAPTER SIXTEEN
CHARAE

Sometimes, I felt like all of this shit was my fault. Like, maybe if I wouldn't have walked out on them things wouldn't have gotten so out of control and off track. Shit was bad back in the day, but it was nowhere near as bad as it is now. I loved Dom and I still to this day love him and the boys, but that life style isn't what I wanted after I got clean. Back when I got on drugs, I was a very vulnerable, lonely, and confused woman. I knew that my husband loved me, but how could he love me the way he swore he did when he chose the streets over me? What made it even worse was when he had come home with Semaj and basically told me that I was going to have to raise him. He treated me like shit and I was the only woman who had his back. Don't get me wrong, when he brought Semaj to me and I began to raise him, I fell in love with him and treated him like he was my own, but that didn't stop the aching pain that I felt in my heart. I was alone, and how the hell was I supposed to feel that way when I had a husband that lived under the same roof as me? We slept together every night in each other's arms but I'd still felt alone. I tried to get his attention and let him know that he was losing me and I was slowly but surely losing myself, but he just expected me to be strong like I always was. Everyone expected me to be strong when I was the one who'd been broken and hurt. I was very weak and at that point I had to find something to help me cope, and that was the drugs that Dom brought to the house.

I'd take some of the drugs from his basement and smoke it, and we'd argue because he thought I was taking the drugs and getting rid of them just so that he could leave the streets alone. I did well with covering up the real deal because he had no idea I was smoking it until he caught me one day. I never knew he cared until he snatched the pipe from my lips, jacked me up like one of his crackheads on the streets, and took me in for a long, tight, loving hug. A hug that I had needed way before I got addicted to that crack. He broke down and seeing him like that broke my heart. By that time, crack was the only thing that could heal me so I left home and got into the streets, not caring about the kids, my household or anything for that matter. I just needed that one thing that could cure my pain. I know that I broke Dom's heart because he always put me on the highest pedestal, but he really pushed me to it. When he tried to convince me that he'd leave the streets alone if I came back home and got help, I didn't believe him so I took my time with the drugs. Even though I know I wasn't living right, I was feeling right and that's all I cared about at the time.

It wasn't until Chazae was twelve years old and he started roaming the streets looking for me. Every single day he'd come to whichever crack house I was in and beg me to come back home. I didn't care to listen until one particular night he came under the bridge where I was and broke down in tears.

It was a cold night in December when me and my other crackhead friends were under the bridge enjoying our fresh hits. We got high, laughed, and talked just like any other normal people.

"If Dom knew his workers were serving you, that nigga would kill everybody around this bitch," my friend, Monique said to me.

Johnazia Gray & *Danielle Offett*

"Dom ain't gone do shit because he ain't gone know shit." I laughed.

I saw a tall young boy walking up and I thought it was just another dealer. I went to my bag to grab the last few dollars I had to cop some more drugs only to be greeted by my son. No matter how high or drunk I was, I admired his handsome little ass. He looked exactly like me and I knew he was going to be just like his dog ass daddy.

"Chazae, I thought you was a dealer. What you doing under the bridge this time of night?" I asked him.

"Mama, please, man. Please come home. Why you out here doing this shit like you don't have a family who wants you?" Tears fell down his face.

"Son, you need to go home. I'm okay. For real," I tried to convince him and myself.

"No, look at you. You're skinny, Ma. You've never looked like this before. Please come home. I can't even sleep at night knowing you out here killing yourself." He grabbed my hands and put them in his.

I wiped away the tear that threatened to fall from my eyes. "I'm sorry, Chazae, but I can't do it. I'm not there yet. This is the only thing that helps me. Your father did this."

"My daddy loves you and you know it and even if you feel that way, me and Maj need you. We still want you."

Chazae was always a hard rock. A stubborn boy he was, so to hear him say all of those things to me softened my heart. It wasn't enough to convince me to come back home though. That wasn't my home.

"Zae, go home."

He shook his head, dropped my hands, and wiped his tears.

TILT MY CROWN TO THE STREETS
Johnazia Gray & *Danielle Offett*

"If I leave this time, I'm washing my fucking hands with you, Ma. I'm never looking for you again and you're in this shit on your own. I can't stress myself out, man. I'm just a little nigga."

"Your daddy should be the one trying to help me. Not you."

"He's tried to help! Pops has done everything to get you to come home and you always leave in the middle of the night and run back to these dirty ass streets. Why don't you love us? What the fuck is wrong with you?" He shook me by my shoulders and cried

I shrugged him off and looked away. What was wrong with me? Dom hurt me so much that this is how I coped.

"What's tomorrow, Ma?"

"Huh?"

"You don't even know what day of the week it is do you?"

"I don't and I don't care, Chazae!" I yelled with tears falling from my eyes. "Damn! Just take your ass home to your lying, cheating ass daddy!"

"Tomorrow's my thirteenth birthday." He shook his head. "I'm done, Ma. Take care of yourself out here." He kissed my cheek and took off running.

I wanted to scream for him to come back but I couldn't. I couldn't say anything. All I could do was cry. How could I miss the birthday of my first born?

I sat down next to my friends and rocked back and forth.

"Your ass is crazy, Charae. If I had a family to go home to I'd get my shit together. You better before it's too damn late," Monique said, firing up her pipe. "Since you're going through it, I guess you can hit my shit. Just don't make it a habit."

Days after that happened, I finally felt the urge to get my shit together. I wanted Chazae to come back for me and motivate me how he did that night, but he'd meant what he said when he said he was done with me. Dom had given up on trying to help me when I turned down his offers long before Chazae stepped in, so I eventually I had to motivate myself and do it on my own. I checked myself into a six-month rehab center and got myself together. It was hard and I was attempted to check myself out a million times but each time, I saw that look on Chazae's face that night under the bridge.

After getting clean, I promised myself that I was going to go back to school and do something constructive with my life, and being an attorney was what I wanted to do. Before all the bullshit, I had already started and passed most of the required classes so it was nothing to pick up where I had left off. I wasn't doing it to be a snitch, but I knew that one day Dom would need me and just like I thought, he ended up needing me. I didn't care to take others down; it was him and my son that I wanted to protect and keep out from those damn cages.

I was from the hood and I knew the good niggas that was into the game and those were the ones that I didn't go after. It was the men that were nasty as fuck and a disgrace to mankind. The ones who silently snitched for a quick come up and set the good niggas up. Those were the ones I focused on taking down. Even though I knew my ex-husband was the biggest dealer in New Orleans, in my eyes, he was untouchable. Hell, in everyone's eyes he was untouchable. He was a very smart man and that was why nobody could touch him. That was why I was so surprised that he got caught up in the bullshit he was in now.

A lot of people that I worked with and worked for had no idea that I was married to Dom before, and that we had kids together, and that was none of their business. That was why I chose to cut ties with Dom and Chazae. I had to in order to keep our relationship off the radar. I actually didn't even have a man or anyone in that field because I didn't need anyone getting close to me and learning about my family. I wasn't in my family circle, but it was my business to protect them from the law. I made sure to look over Dom's and my son's operation.

Chazae hated me because he looked at me as if I was a snitch, but I had actually been looking out for them. If I was a nasty bitch, I could've been had them put away for good, but there was no way in hell I could do that. That was my son and basically my only love. I loved Chazae, but for him to think I was going to kiss his ass for the rest of his life for doing what I felt was best for me was a no. His own father didn't treat me like shit and neither did Semaj before he was killed, so yes, the way Chazae treated me broke my heart in more ways than one. I wish that he hadn't seen me caught up in my drug act when he was younger, but that was something I just couldn't change. I indeed had fucked up in the past, but I wasn't going to allow anyone to remind me of that, and that was another reason I stayed away from Chazae.

I was very surprised when I found out that Chazae was even in the mix of that drug bullshit with his father because he saw what it had done to me. He had turned out in a way I had no idea he would've and that hurt too. He was a mean young man. Very stern and stubborn like me, so I knew what the deal was when it came to us getting a mother and son bond. It would take a lot for us but I knew it would happen someday. Because I am the mother I tried, but after several attempts and continuously being disrespected, I stepped back.

Having a bond with Semaj was a good thing and he still made me feel like a mother before he left this world. My heart hurt because he was the one who treated me like someone. When he got older, he wanted me to still be a part of his life and I appreciated that from him. When Chazae wouldn't let me help him with the funeral, I promised myself that I wasn't kissing his ass anymore. He was caught up in his emotions and basically letting the devil win. I promised to have one final sit down with him after I left from seeing his father and if that didn't go right, I was going to step back again.

I sat in the same private room that I had sat in a million times and played with my nails. It was very cold, and I couldn't wait to get back home and make me a hot bowl of chili and sit in front of my fireplace. Most people would call me old and bitter since I only went to work and home and didn't have a man, but that was really by choice. The loyalty I had for Dom and my ungrateful ass son was buried inside of me and wasn't going anywhere. It was them or nothing and I owed them that much.

The doors opened and I stood and adjusted my dress. When Dom walked into the room, I had to bite my bottom lip. His face was freshly trimmed, he had a fresh haircut, and those beautiful thick eye brows and full eyelashes did something to little ole me. He smiled, showing off those perfectly white teeth, making my old ass pearl gates fly right open.

"Charae?" He leaned over the table and kissed my cheek.

"Dom." I kissed his cheek back.

"So, is this a personal visit or are you back here on business?" he asked me.

I smiled and giggled. "A little of both."

He nodded his head and rubbed his hands over his face. "I still feel the same, Rae. I ain't testifying on nobody. So if that's what you're here for, you can keep it moving."

"Shhh." I put my finger over my lip. "That's not what I'm here for."

He looked down at my finger and smiled at the sight of the shiny rock. "I see you put your ring back on your ring finger."

I smiled like a school girl and tucked one of my dreads behind my ear. "If you can get out of here and let the streets go, I'll give it all up."

"Huh?" he asked, almost yelling. Clearly, he had been caught off guard.

"You heard me. You see, Dom, when I chose my career, I knew what it was I was doing. I chose this career to protect you from ending up in here. I mean, I didn't know that I was going to have to protect my son from this bullshit too, but that's just what it turned out to be. You've never been touched because I hadn't allowed you to be touched. You've been safe and the law hasn't been on your ass because I made sure that you were untouchable. I know that you're a smart man and you had enough power to not be touched on your own, but don't think your name has never been brought to me. It's been mentioned, just not how it's been lately and the only reason it was mentioned this time is because they have a little evidence on you."

Dom sat there in deep thought. "I can't believe this shit, Charae. So you're telling me you did all this attorney shit for us? Is that right?"

As expected, he was a little hesitant but I could tell he was hearing me out.

"I did it because I felt that I owed y'all that much for walking out on y'all back then. Don't get me wrong, Dom, you did some fucked up shit to me back in the day and I blamed you for a very long time. But that didn't stop me from loving you. You loved me, you were just younger and you thought money could fix everything. With all this shit going on, I'm tired of running and hiding behind the desk. You hurt me and I hurt you. I want to bury all the hurt, all the pain, and move on with our lives. That's *if* you still love me."

"Damn, Charae." He rubbed his hand over his head. "I'm not gon' lie. I still love you, and I never stopped. I really don't know how to feel. I mean, I'm still fucked up from how you turned your back on me and the boys but I love you. I know I played a big part in why you did what you did back then, and I'm man enough now to admit that shit. Like you said, I was a young, rich nigga that did some stupid shit. I don't know when and I don't know if we ever will, but I hope we can make this shit right. I know that it was a lot of shit that I wish I could change from our past and I owe you so much. Before you left me for the streets, you were a really good woman. I'm so sorry." He put his hands on top of mine. "I would love to get out and start shit over with us, but I know for a fact they're going to throw the book at my black ass."

He didn't know it, but his apology and lifting some of the guilt that I'd carried around for years off my shoulders meant a lot to me.

"Just be prepared to walk out of here in two weeks." I stood and winked.

"Two weeks? How the fuck is that possible?" he asked me.

"Anything is possible when you have the right connections. I'll make a way out of no way for my family, Dom. No matter what the situation is. And I have that much power."

Johnazia Gray & Danielle Offett

From the smile on his face, I could tell I had just made his entire day. I could see the love and admiration in his eyes that he used to have for me. Maybe us having a happy ever after could happen after all.

"I don't know what type of strings you're about to pull, but thank you, Charae. If you can pull this off, I won't be able to thank you enough."

I winked at him flirtatiously. "I can think of a few ways you can thank me, but we can save that for another time."

His eyes roamed my body and he let out a sexy chuckle. "Let me find out my ole lady is still a freak after all these years."

This man still had that effect on me. The cobwebs immediately began to fall after hearing those words. I had to clench my thighs together.

"On that note, our visit time is over. I will always have your back. Now I got to make things right with that son of mine. I'm not sure how easy that'll be, but I'ma try."

"That nigga might as well get used to this shit because you're back now. He'll understand if you tell him what you just told me about your career."

"Even if it that wasn't the reason, I'm the mother and that boy needs to learn to respect me."

He put his hands up in mock surrender. "You're right. Make him put some respek on ya name," he said in his best Birdman voice.

I couldn't help but laugh. He was always a fucking clown.

"Well, give me a hug before I leave. I'll be back to visit tomorrow."

When Dom stood up, he leaned over and gave me the most passionate kiss that I had received in years. It made me feel so warm on the inside.

Johnazia Gray & *Danielle Offett*

"On the real though, thank you, Charae. I need you to do me a favor too. This is Semaj's girlfriend sister's address. Last time I heard, she hadn't been doing well. Please go over there and check on them for me. Those are some really good girls and I'm worried about their well-being. Chazae can be cutthroat sometimes. You know his ass is rude and might be over there telling her to suck that shit up and boss up. I'm sure it would be good for them to have gentle comfort from a woman."

I looked down at the paper and nodded my head. That was the least I could do for my late son. Too bad we had to meet under these circumstances.

***

Chazae walked into Drago's Restaurant looking exactly like me with his father's skin tone. I could tell he hadn't slept in days from the black bags under his pretty eyes. I stood and opened my arms for a hug only to be frowned at.

"Okay," I said to myself.

"What's up?" He sat next to me at the bar, getting straight to the point.

"That's not how you greet your mama, Chazae. It's 'bout time you stop acting like that toward me."

"If this is a family reunion, say that shit so I can leave. I got more important things to do." He waved the bartender down. "Let me get two shots of Ciroc and a Redbull."

"Make that four shots, please sir," I told the bartender.

It had been a minute since I'd had a drink, but I knew meeting with him wasn't going to go well sober. This was straight up rude and cocky, a combination that didn't mix.

"So what's up forreal, Charae? It must be an emergency for you to keep blowing me up."

"Your father is coming home," I told him with a smile.

The frown that formed on his face was unexpected. I thought he would be the most happy to hear the news.

"That nigga in there fucking snitching?"

"Boy, shut your young, dumb ass up. I believe that you'll snitch before your father would. Better act like you know."

"You got the wrong, nigga. I'll lay down and do my time before I ever tell."

"Okay and your father would too so shut up. You're always talking shit like you know everything but you really don't know shit, *little boy*. Just be quiet, listen, and order yourself another shot because you're gonna piss me off and that old quiet Charae that I've been giving you is out the fucking window." I looked him directly into his eyes. "Don't let the suit and briefcase fool you, baby boy."

"Let me get another shot, bruh," he told the bartender. "And another thing, I don't really have respect for your ass so I won't mind cursing you back out. I don't know where this new attitude came from, but remember I'm still the same nigga and I give no fucks. Especially about you." He looked me up and down.

This was the same look of hatred and disgust that he had given me back in the day under the bridge, when he begged me to come home for the last time. I immediately felt like shit but refused to back down from him. Not this time. It was time I get my son back; my son and not this damn, rude ass boy.

"I'm the reason your father is coming home, and before you start talking shit to me, I didn't snitch either. I worked some things out," I told him, hoping to lighten up the situation.

"How you worked some things out if you and him ain't snitching? You one of those crooked attorneys or some shit?" he asked.

"Maybe, but only crooked for y'all asses."

"What you mean by that, lady?"

As much as I wanted to get up and walk away, I decided that I couldn't keep running away from my problems with this boy. I was one of the reasons he acted this way and I had to get myself together.

I sat there for almost an hour explaining to him why I chose to be a state attorney. After each explanation I gave, he shot back another question as if he didn't believe me, but I had no reason to lie so I answered them with ease. I wasn't surprised that he was shocked and still choosing to be an asshole though.

"Damn, man. If what you're saying is true, that's crazy as fuck." He threw his drink back.

"I'm not lying about it. I have nothing to lie to you about, Chazae."

"I hear you, but I still don't trust you and I don't know you, Charae. So excuse me if I'm not as easily convinced like my love struck ass pops."

There was an awkward silence as we both threw back shots. I told him everything he needed and wanted to know. If that wasn't enough, I was out of options.

"Prove yourself."

"What?" I looked at him as if he had two heads.

"Prove yourself. If you did this for me and my pops, prove it."

"And how am I supposed to do that?"

"Get all the information on that cat that took my daddy down so I can handle him."

"No! I don't have to do that. Either you believe me or you don't."

"How I know you're not trying to get close to me to take me down, Charae? How can you just expect to come back in a nigga's life, say you did this for us, and expect me to just forgive you? You do know that you're the biggest attorney ever right now, right? You send niggas like me up the creek every day."

"I know that." I nodded my head.

"And you do know that if I open up to you about one little thing your ass can take me down for life, right? Why should I set myself up for some shit like that?"

"If I wanted to do that, I could've been did that. I just need you to trust me. I'm not giving you Odney's information because I don't need you to get in deeper shit and fuck my plan up. I'm not here to take you down. Like I said before, if I wanted to do that I would've been did that and I wouldn't be getting your father out of all this shit! You honestly don't have any other choice because you two are hot as fish grease so like it or not, I'm your fucking savior. If you don't want to tell me anything, fine, but I'm still going to do what I have to do as your mother to protect you."

He nodded his head. "I guess we'll see, Charae."

"What you used to call me when you was younger?"

"Ma." He threw his another shot back.

"I would like it if you called me that from now on. I'ma give you a few weeks to tie up your loose ends in the streets, and then you're going to start a business or some shit because I'm retiring from this business when your dad comes home. If I don't, I'ma end up going down with y'all asses."

"And what makes you think you're going to go down?"

Johnazia Gray & Danielle Offett

"Because I know shit is going to get real messy and with me about to help y'all, I can possibly get in a shitload of trouble, but I won't get in any trouble if I go ahead and retire."

"Just because you retire don't mean your ass won't get in trouble. You ain't as smart as I thought you was." He chuckled.

"And you're as stupid as I think you are if you think I don't have connections. Just trust me on this, please."

I placed my hand on top of his and looked directly in his eyes. He stared back into them as if trying to read me. After a few seconds, he removed his hand from mine and looked away.

"I guess I'll follow your lead for now just don't try any slick shit. Mother or not–"

I cut him off. I didn't need to hear the rest of his statement.

"What you know about Semaj's girlfriend? Your father wanted me to stop by and check on her. I can only imagine how she's feeling."

He shook his head. "Derria is family. She's doing bad as fuck though. Niggas in the hood said she's been trying to cop drugs and everything, man. I told each and every last one of them muthafuckas they better not sell her shit. Don't even supply her a pack of gum. Send her my way if she needs something."

Just looking at him, I could tell he was not only fucked up about Semaj's death for himself, but for the sake of Derria too.

"I feel bad for her, but she needs to tighten the fuck up. She can't turn weak because Semaj wouldn't want that shit. They were really in love. Those two were always on some lovey dovey type shit and I used to clown his ass." He chuckled. "They were so in love, they encouraged me to open my heart up and shit."

"That's really sad. Maybe I can talk to her and share my story." I shrugged. I knew firsthand what it was like to turn to drugs to cope with life.

"Maybe." He shrugged his shoulders. "Just don't encourage her to continue to smoke that shit as an excuse like you did. Encourage her to get off of it. I'd hate to have to start taking off my watches when I see her ass."

We both laughed at his joke.

"You're a true asshole, li'l boy. You know that?"

He chuckled. "That's what I've heard."

"You want to ride over there with me? You know them more than I do."

"Hell nah. I don't want to be nowhere near her snake ass sister."

"Why not?"

"That bitch set up my fucking brother and I'ma kill her ass too. Just waiting for the right time." His jaw clenched in anger.

As much as I wanted Chazae to open up to me and get a comfortable bond with me, I knew it was going to take some time. I really wanted him to know that I knew much more about him and his crew than he thought. Semaj told me everything due to him being such a mama's boy, and I hated to break the news to Semaj, but he didn't know his circle how he thought he did.

"That girl is innocent. Who needs to be handled is that fucking Tauris because he's the one behind all of this. That girl didn't know shit about what Semaj and her baby's daddy had going on."

"What the fuck?" he asked. "How you know this?"

"Semaj came to me and told me how Tauris linked him into doing business with him and his cousin, and he didn't like the nigga because he was foul. Something about how he saw him at Derria's sister house one day, but Derria's sister wasn't even fucking with him like that. Trust me, she was just as clueless. Don't fault her for the doings of a snake."

"Wow. That explains a fucking lot. That's why that nigga went missing, huh?"

I nodded my head.

"Damn, I owe Dola a big ass apology, man."

The fact that he cared enough to apologize said a lot about how he felt toward this Dola girl. There was no way I was going to let him mess it up over a misunderstanding.

"Come with me and give it to her." I reached over and rubbed his face.

He gently moved my hands off of his face and shook his head.

"Give me my time, Charae. Don't force it." His voice cracked.

I had no choice but to respect that we weren't there yet. When tears came to his eyes, my heart was broken.

"That nigga grew up with us. I knew something wasn't right, man. He'd been acting funny as fuck for a minute now. Fuck!" He banged his massive hands on the bar causing the other parties to look on. "I should've looked more into it and knocked his ass off before it got this far. Him and his fucking peoples."

"You should just let me put their whole team away," I suggested.

"Jail time? Nah, those niggas gone be doing graveyard time when I catch up with them. Those niggas killed my brother. Tauris must've forgot what happens to those who betray me. The grim reaper is coming for that ass."

The look in his eyes was very dark and cold. I'd represented some ruthless people but never had I gotten chills like I got from looking into the eyes of my own son.

"Let's go get my woman back before the madness starts back up."

CHAPTER SEVENTEEN

DERRIA

My niece sat in the front of me wanting to play as I lay back on the sofa, lost in my thoughts about Semaj. Tears welled up in my eyes and my head began to pound. It was almost a month since he'd been gone and it still felt so fresh. It weighed so heavy on my heart that I could feel it pouring out of my chest.

"Titi, why you not playing *paddy cake* with me?" Princess frowned.

"Princess, leave me alone!" I yelled.

When Princess jumped and began to cry, it made me cry. I hadn't meant to react like that, but it was just my nerves. From my supposed to be husband's death to my own issues, I was fucked up in the head and couldn't deal with myself or Princess.

"My God, Derria! Don't talk to her like that. I understand you're going through things but this is still a chile." Ms. Shirley put the blanket she was knitting down and sat Princess in her lap. The side eye she gave me didn't go unnoticed, but I was too depressed to reply.

I wiped away the tears that continuously rolled down my face. I wanted to feel better. I wanted to be my old self but it felt like that was impossible. There was no way I could feel the same with Semaj gone. I looked down at my ring and burst into tears. Nobody could do or say anything to make me feel better. The one guy that pushed me, motivated me, and loved me for me was gone and I was never getting him back. I got tired of people preaching to me telling me that it was going to be all right when I knew that it wasn't. I knew that being dead was better than being alive and feeling the way I feel. This feeling hurt my soul and it made me miserable. Even drugs couldn't make me feel better, at least not permanently. I've tried everything and nothing cured this broken heart and emptiness that I felt.

"Go to your room and let me talk to your auntie, baby," Ms. Shirley said to Princess.

"It's okay, Mama Shirley. I want to sit right here with her until she feels better." Princess sat next to me and gently rubbed my back.

She was such a sweet little girl. I loved her to death but everything she was doing was irritating me. I didn't want to feel the way I was feeling toward her but I couldn't help it.

"Do what she said, Princess, and do it now!" I yelled at her, causing her to burst out in tears.

Dola walked into the front door with a shitload of grocery bags. She immediately dropped them when she saw Princess crying.

"What's wrong with my baby?" She frowned.

"Derria keeps yelling at her." Shirley shook her head and continued to knit her blanket.

Dola looked at me and took a deep breath. "Derria, I understand what you're going through, sis, but you're going to have to control yourself. My baby hasn't done anything wrong. Please don't take your anger and hurt out on her."

"No, you don't." I shook my head and wiped the tears.

"What?"

"You don't understand what I'm going through, Dola, so stop saying that fake ass shit. Just stop it!" I yelled.

I got tired of everyone telling me that they understood and that everything would be okay. How? They had never been through this shit. They had never felt this pain. *Never!*

"Go to your room, P," Dola told her.

Princess slowly walked down the hall after giving me an unwanted hug. "I love you, Auntie. It's going to be okay," she turned around and said.

That only made me cry harder.

Dola sat next to me and dropped her head. I knew she was broken because I was and I hated that, but I couldn't help myself. She might as well get used to it because this was going to be me. I just grew to accept it. I was going to be a young, depressed, miserable ass bitch.

"Derria, look at me." She turned my head and scanned my face. "Have you been taking your depression pills like the doctor told you?"

"I don't want those," I told her.

"You have to take them, Sissy. That's the only thing that's going to help you cope."

I shook my head and looked down at my trembling hands. I hadn't had a hit since I got out of the hospital and the withdrawal symptoms hadn't stopped.

"Derria, please, *please* don't give up on yourself like this. I can't take it. I'm going to lose my mind if you don't find yours. You know besides my baby you're all I got." She cried. I could hear her sniffling but I was too ashamed to look at her.

Ms. Shirley cleared her throat.

"Besides you, my baby, and Ms. Shirley. I'm sorry," she corrected herself. "I've given it all up just to nurture you back to health. You can't give up on yourself like this."

"You quit the fucking club? Why would you do that?"

"Because you need to be looked after. At all times. I don't need you overdosing again. I have enough money for us to survive."

"Enough for you to survive. I'm already dead inside."

"I checked your grades online," she said, sadly.

"And?"

"You're failing, Derria! You haven't been going to school, you haven't been doing your assignments, and you haven't even thought to reach out to your teachers. You're just going to let it all go like that? I worked so hard for you to succeed. *You* worked so hard to succeed. Are you really going to let everything we've done to get you here be done in vain?"

"You see what I'm saying? My boyfriend just died and you think I'm thinking about fucking school, Dola? I don't give a fuck 'bout none of this shit!" I jumped up from the couch and screamed like a mad woman. That was exactly how I felt. I picked up the tall African vase that sat in the middle of her coffee table and hurled it against the wall. "My life is over. My fiancé is dead and you want me to focus on school. Why? Is it because you popped your pussy to put me through it?"

Before I could even continue, Dola jumped in my face and slapped me so hard I stumbled. I was shocked but my heart hurt worse than the stinging of my cheek.

"You won't disrespect me, Derria! I don't know what has gotten into you but disrespect is what you're not gonna do! I'm just here trying to help you. I'm not against you and I'm not your enemy!" She shook me and cried. "It's us against the world, Sissy. Remember?"

I was struggling with myself. I knew she was hurting and that I was the cause of it, but my pain wouldn't allow me to care.

"Get off of me! Just leave me alone!" I yanked away from her and ran out of the house.

"Derria!" Dola yelled, running outside behind me.

I ran through the projects without looking back. The more I heard her call for me, the faster I ran. I just needed to get away.

She was right; she hadn't done anything to me. She hadn't done nothing to me at all, but I couldn't control the way I felt. I couldn't fake being happy when I was clearly sad and broken. I was fucked up. For real. I wanted Semaj. I wanted to wake up from this stupid uncalled for ass nightmare. It was all too much for my little heart and mind. I wanted him, but I knew for a fact that I couldn't have him.

I walked a few buildings over where the dope boys and trap niggas usually hung at. I needed something to smoke. Anything just to make me feel better for the moment. My chest was hurting from the heartache and I needed something quick to handle me. I knew a drink was going to take too long and I didn't have time.

"What's up, Ma?" One of the dudes that was shooting dice came over to me and asked.

"What you got?" I got straight to the point.

"What you want?"

"Something good and strong."

I had tried cocaine once and it wasn't so bad. I could use some of that but I wasn't fucking with any needles.

"This." He smiled and dangled a bag of coke in front of me, and my eyes lit up like a Christmas tree.

"Yeah." I smiled and went into my pockets. My hands were shaking in anticipation of getting the product in my hands. When I looked up to give him the money, he was sucker punched in the face so hard it made him fall straight back on his ass.

"Don't you ever fucking serve her, nigga! Are you crazy?" Chazae began to stomp him out. "You got a death wish, little nigga?"

Johnazia Gray & *Danielle Offett*

My eyes almost popped out my head when the niggas the guy had just been playing dice with helped Chazae out. I screamed at the top of my lungs for them to stop, but my cries were ignored. When they were done with him, that nigga was out cold. He was a bloody ass mess and I was pissed that Chazae had come and fucked shit up.

My anger went out the window when I saw the little baggie a few steps away. Like a cat, I scrambled over to pick it up only for a large Timberland boot to come smashing down on it. I looked up into Chazae's menacing eyes. The look would've scared most, but I was more pissed that he messed up my chances of getting high. I tried to push his leg off of it but his massive frame made it impossible.

"Why the fuck would you do that, Chazae? He didn't even do nothing!" I yelled at him with tears in my eyes.

He grabbed my arm and power-walked back toward my sister's building.

"Chazae, you don't have to grab her like that! Let her walk by herself," an older woman yelled, following us.

He ignored her and continued to drag me toward the building. When we got to the stairs, he pushed me up against the wall.

"What the fuck, Derria? You really out here living like this?" He looked hurt.

"Like what, Chazae?"

"You was just about to buy coke from that nigga and you scrambled around trying to find it on your knees like a fucking crackhead. Tell me you ain't rocking like that, man."

When he looked me in my eyes, it felt like he was burning a hole through my soul. I couldn't deal so I turned away and did what I knew best—cried.

"Man, stop all that fucking cryin!" he barked, only making me cry harder.

He took a deep breath and shook his head. "I know you hurting, Ma, but you can't just give up on your life. You can't."

"But he's gone, Chazae. He's gone. It wasn't supposed to happen like this," I cried and sat on the steps.

"I know, man." He sat next to me and put his head in his hands.

"Who is she?" I nodded toward the lady who stood in front of us with tears in her eyes.

"Oh, that's Charae. Charae, this is Derria. The one my daddy told you to come and check up on."

"This is your mother?" I asked him to be sure.

"Something like that." He shrugged.

"Excuse him, darling. Yes, I'm his mother. He's just acting like a childish little boy right now, but Dom did send me over here to see about you. Do you mind if we come inside so I can sit down and talk with you?"

Charae was a beautiful woman. I swore that Chazae looked exactly like his father but that quickly changed once I laid eyes on this beautiful woman. She was brown-skinned with the most beautiful exotic eyes. Her thighs and hips were so damn thick, giving me a full view of her ass from the sides. Her long, thick, beautiful dreads were styled into a Mohawk. She was beautiful and she looked nothing like the crackhead from back in the day that Semaj had told me about. As I thought of Dom, I figured they'd make a very nice couple.

Wow, I thought.

"Can we just talk out here? My sister and I just got into it and I'm not trying to face her right now."

"Nah, let's go inside because I need to talk to Dola too," Chazae said.

"Chazae, my sister had nothing to do with that. If you're trying to make her feel bad, then just leave. I'm breaking her enough," I told him.

I massaged my skull and counted to ten over and over again in my head like the therapist told me to. I knew my blood pressure was high because I felt horrible.

"I know she didn't do it. Come on." He tapped my thigh and walked upstairs.

I sighed and followed him. "You can come in," I told his mother.

I hated that she had to see me like this, but I didn't care. It wasn't like I was going to be marrying her son. That was over. My dream was ruined so I didn't have to put on for anyone. This was me and they were going to have to accept it.

Chazae knocked on the door and Dola snatched it open.

"Siss–" she stopped dead in her tracks when she saw Chazae standing there.

"Fuck no, nigga. Get the fuck from in front of my door!" She pushed him. "Last time I saw you, you threatened to put a bullet in my head. Mama Shirley, go get me your gun!"

"Man, chill out." He grabbed her hand and gently pushed her inside of the house. "I didn't come here for all that."

"Derria, why'd you bring him here?" she asked.

"I didn't bring him here, shit. I was out there trying to buy me something to fucking smoke and he came and fucked that up."

"Smoke? Nah, don't make that shit sound so fucking innocent, you were out there trying to buy some fucking dope!" He yelled at me. The look of disgust was all over his face. For the longest, Chazae had looked at me as the good girl. He had to understand that shit had changed.

"What?" Dola looked at me in disbelief. I didn't care though.

"He's telling the truth." I shrugged.

She sucked her teeth and shook her head.

"Sit down and let me talk to you, Dola." Chazae grabbed her hand and looked at her with pleading eyes.

He looked at her how Semaj used to look at me when he'd fucked up. The way he looked into her eyes to get to her soul was magical. He had love for her. The way he touched her and massaged the top of her hands with his thumbs made my eyes water. They were going to get together. I knew it. I could feel it and I was going to be left out. Miserable and lonely. I was jealous for sure. Just from the looks he was giving her.

"Who's your guest, Chazae?" Ms. Shirley asked.

"I'm his mother. I'm sorry. How are you?" She shook Ms. Shirley's hand.

"I'll be okay once my girls get back to normal," she said.

"Are you their mother?" Charae asked.

"No, but I'm something close to it."

Charae nodded her head in understanding.

"I'm sorry. It's nice to meet you." Dola stood.

"Nice to meet y'all too, baby." Charae nodded. "Handle your business, Chazae." She looked at him.

"I was wrong. You didn't have anything to do with what happened to my little nigga and I'm so sorry."

"I told you I didn't. I'm not that type of person." Her eyes watered. "Why couldn't you believe me?"

"I'm sorry, Dola. You have to understand, I'm a street nigga and when shit like that happens I have to raise red flags. I don't trust women and I was open to you about that. When I snapped on you, I didn't think shit through and that was whack as fuck on my part."

"How'd you know that what I said was true?" she asked him. "What made you change your mind now?"

"Semaj opened up to Charae about a few things that let me know that this had nothing to do with you."

Tears dropped from Dola's eyes and she nodded her head. "Well, I told you I didn't have anything to do with that. You chose to treat me the way you did, so whatever." She shrugged.

"Can I make it up to you?" he asked.

"No, Chazae. Right now, all I want to do is focus on taking care of my sister. She needs me more than I need you and your bullshit. You see her."

She pointed at me.

When everyone looked at me in pity, I felt ashamed. I felt like shit and I knew I looked even worse.

"Okay, stop looking at me please," I snapped.

"See, I have to get her back to her normal loving self. You know this isn't her. I just want to focus on my sister's wellbeing. I'm so sorry for what happened to Semaj but it's nothing you can do for me. I tried hard to show you that my loyalty was with you and you shitted on me. So no, Chazae. You can't make it up to me no kind of way."

"I'm not taking no for an answer though, Ma. I understand why you feel the way you feel but I can't let you forget about a nigga and keep it moving."

"Well, you are today." She stood and opened the door. When she stood by it and looked at him, he looked sad.

"Come on, Charae," he told her.

"I have to talk to Derria though, Chazae."

Johnazia Gray & Danielle Offett

"No need, ma'am. Try again some other time." Shirley shook her head at Charae.

Charae looked at me with sad eyes and said, "Please call me if you need to talk or anything. You need something? Is there anything I can do for you?"

"I'm okay. Thank you," I lied.

"Okay." She walked behind Chazae.

"Give him a chance, darling." She hugged Dola.

When they left, Dola walked down the hall and cried like a baby.

"You need to get it together, Derria. Do it for us," Ms. Shirley said. "Come walk upstairs with me so I can rub you down with some of this holy oil and pray over you."

As negative as I felt, I couldn't deny that I needed prayer. I needed prayer and a hit from somebody. That's a bad, sinful combination but I felt like I needed them both right now. I just prayed that Chazae didn't have all the niggas in the hood scared to serve me. I thought about my sister who was broken and I wanted to go back there and make her feel better, but I couldn't. Hell, I couldn't even make myself feel better. I just accepted the fact that this was my life.

CHAPTER EIGHTEEN

CHAZAE

Women. Can't live with them and damn sure can't live without them. I went from saying fuck the world and riding for my niggas, to saying these niggas ain't really my niggas, and keeping the women in my life closer. Even though I lost my brother behind this street shit, it brought three women in my life that I would die for.

Charae, or Ma as she wanted me to call her, was the woman who caused me so much hurt and pain since I was a little nigga. She was the reason I said fuck love and fuck bitches, but now that she was trying to come back around, I felt my heart repairing itself. I was still rude as fuck to her at times when I had flashbacks, but I was working on it. I would never admit that I only wanted a mother's love because that would be some sucka shit, but I will say that having her apologize and proving herself by riding for the family showed me that she was really in it for the right reasons. It had been a week since she promised to get my father out and from what the lawyers were saying, things were starting to look up. I didn't know what type of shit she had going on, but she was the fucking truth! Evidence was disappearing and witnesses were getting amnesia. The key witness, Odney muthafuckin' Romos, was still fucking missing and I was getting frustrated looking for his ass. Charae said she was on top of it, but this was a nigga that wouldn't be found if he didn't want to. I was determined to step in. I had until the end of the week to find him and silence him forever.

TILT MY CROWN TO THE STREETS
Johnazia Gray & Danielle Offett

Dola and Derria had been brought into my life all thanks to Semaj. If it hadn't been for Derria, I never would have gotten a chance to lay eyes on Dola's fine ass. I knew I hurt and pushed her away, but I was a broken nigga. Niggas can be broken and fucked up in the head too. I was used to doing, "Wam-Bam, thank you, ma'ams," not actually feeling a bitch. Me threatening to kill her pushed her further away from me, but I was determined to get her back. That day me and Charae left her apartment, I had given her space but only for the rest of the day. The following day, I started back popping up at her house with breakfast and flowers every day. Some corny ass shit, right? I didn't give a fuck because I would do anything to get her back as my woman. Her reason was because she wanted to focus on Derria so I decided to help her with Derria. I mean, she was my little sister too.

Since Charae had so much in common with her and could relate to her pain and daily struggles, she had been spending the most time with her. It was working but she still needed professional help. Somehow, she convinced her to get checked into a rehab program. Since Semaj was the cause of this, I felt it was only right that I be the one to pay for it and drop her off today.

Pulling up to Dola's building, Derria was already outside sitting on the stairs. I jumped out the car and gave her a hug.

"Wassup, Sis?" I greeted, taking her bags.

"Can we take my car? I'm not in the mood for that speedy ass race car."

I decided to bring out my all black Lexus FLA since it was a special occasion, but clearly she wasn't feeling it. I looked over at her red 2016 Toyota Camry and frowned. It was some girly shit, but I sucked it up and walked with her toward the car and put the bags in the trunk.

You ready?" I asked her.

She let out a deep sigh. "As ready as I'm going to be. I hate feeling this way so I know I have get myself together. Not only for me but for Dola and Semaj. I know he's shaking his head at me right now and so is Dola every damn day."

Speaking of Dola, I wondered why she hadn't come outside. She knew I was on the way because I told her. She was still being stubborn but I was gonna break her down slowly. After helping Derria in the car, I took two steps at a time to get to Dola's door. I walked in to find her sitting on the couch painting her toenails.

"Damn, do you knock?" she asked, rolling her eyes.

"Come on, now. You know me better than that," I told her with a smile.

She shook her head and went back to painting her toenails. I walked over, picked her feet up, and sat so that they were in my lap. She looked at me but didn't say a word as I took the toenail polish and began to paint her big toe. I wasn't a feet kind of nigga and had never painted shit in my life, but I was willing to try just to get her to smile at me. I held her big toe in my hand and concentrated as I did baby strokes. It wasn't as hard as it seemed, but I still managed to get polish all on her skin.

Dola laughed and snatched the polish away from me. "Boy, give it to me before you end up painting my damn legs."

"Oh shit! I finally got a smile. That's the shit I like," I told her honestly.

She tooted her lips to the side but I could tell she was trying not to blush. "Whatever, Zae. You're still not out the dog house."

"That's cool. I'll stay in the dog house as long as you slide through and keep me company."

She laughed. "You're so damn crazy."

"Only for you. I'm tired of this cat and mouse game. A nigga fucked up and I'm sorry. I told you a nigga wasn't perfect and you told me you would work with me and ride until the wheels fell off. What happened to that? I'm still seeing three tires and a flat. Let's change that shit and keep it moving," I told her, staring into her brown eyes.

She didn't have to say a word. Her eyes spoke for her and I knew she was still feeling me. I leaned in to kiss her, praying she didn't push me away. Luckily for me, she didn't. As our tongues danced in each other's warm mouths, the oxygen we were losing began to feel unimportant. She began to lean back and I positioned myself between her plump thighs. I slid my hand into the waistband of her tiny boy shorts and landed in a puddle of wetness.

"Damn, you must be ready for a nigga," I told her, stroking her shaved pussy furiously.

She looked down at the bulge and my pants and bit her lip. "Somebody is ready for me too."

Before I could respond, my phone rang. I pulled it out of my pocket and saw that it was Derria. *Shit!* I forgot we had somewhere to be. Dola glanced at the phone as well and smiled.

"Take care of my little sister, please."

"That's my little sis too so don't worry. You just have that ass ready when I get back. You been holding out on a nigga giving me blue balls. It's time to make you work for this dick," I told her, readjusting myself before I kissed her and took off back down the stairs.

I jumped back in the car and smashed down on the gas. "My bad, yo' sister needed help painting her toe nails."

Derria gave me a knowing look and smiled. "Sure, she did. If you want to stay and do the nasty, I can call an Uber."

"Fuck all that. You know I gotchu. You just get ready to kick this shit you got so I don't have to fuck you up."

As we drove, it wasn't long before Derria went to sleep. Recovery Ranch was about an hour's drive but it was nothing to me. As she slept, she looked like the innocent girl that I'd known before life happened. I prayed that these people could help her face her demons and clean herself up. I'd really grown to love her as a sister and I couldn't deal with the Charae situation all over again.

Sounds of my phone ringing brought me back from my own thoughts. It was Big Melo. He knew I was handling shit so it had to be an emergency.

"Speak," I announced.

"Aye, Boss Man, we just found that missing mouth piece."

"Huh?" I asked. Sometimes this speaking in code shit was irritating.

"You remembered that broad ya pops was dealing with, with the loose lips?" he asked.

My ears instantly perked up. "Word?"

"Yup, saw her go in a crib across from my BM house."

I knew exactly where his baby mama stayed.

"Say less. Stay posted," I told him before hanging up.

"Yes!" I yelled, punching the steering wheel. It must've been my lucky day to be catching up to this nigga Odney. He was running and I almost gave up, but the streets always had eyes for a nigga.

Derria stirred and sat up. "What happened?" she asked, clueless.

Johnazia Gray & Danielle Offett

For a minute, I forgot she was in the car. Damn. I calculated the drive to the rehab and we still had an hour to go. But if I got off the highway now, I could make it to Odney in an hour. I debated with myself for a few seconds before cutting through traffic and getting off the exit. I knew it wasn't okay to bring Derria with me, but I had to catch up with a nigga before he made a move.

"Where you going? Damn, Zae! Why are you driving so fast?" she asked, holding on to the door handle for safety.

I eased up on the gas so she could calm down. "My bad. Look, I normally wouldn't do no shit like this but I need you to sit tight while I make a stop."

I was glad when she didn't ask any more questions even though I could read the uncertainty on her face. I didn't have time for twenty-one questions. All I could think about was what I wanted to do to Odney's snake ass.

*****

Pulling up in the neighborhood, I surveyed the block. All seemed to be quiet. I spotted Big Melo's car and parked a couple houses up from it. I shot him a quick text telling him to meet me around back.

"Look, stay here. Don't look at anybody, don't talk to anybody, and don't open the door for anybody."

Before she could respond, I was already out the car and creeping across the street. I used the next house over and then slid my way into the house Odney was in. Once in the backyard, I peeked around to make sure there weren't any alarms. Once I was satisfied, I peeked through each window. He was alone in the living room with his head down to the coffee table.

"This nigga over here putting snow skis up his nose?" Big Melo whispered, peeking through the window. He passed me a pair of gloves matching his own. I slid them on. "We got a minute. I been watching this house all day. A couple undercovers was here about twenty minutes ago. They're most likely checking up on him every hour so we need to make it quick."

"Yup, he knows his time is almost up. Pick the lock," I told him.

He went to work on the backdoor and we had access within seconds. I put my fingers to my lips and slowly cracked the door open. We ducked and tiptoed until we were right next to the living room. We were so close I could hear him breathe. I motioned for him to check all the rooms while I dealt with Odney.

My eyes watched Melo for a minute as he quietly opened up door after door. Things were clear so far, so I entered the living room and leaned up against the wall. His head was now back and he was on cloud nine. He didn't even feel my presence, but I was about to make it known.

"Damn, Odney. Looks like you're about to fulfill your own death wish with all that damn coke," I told him.

In slow motion, his head came forward and our eyes met. He looked like he had seen a ghost.

"You didn't really think you would get away with setting up my old man, now did you?" I asked, rhetorically.

He opened his mouth to speak but I put my hand up.

"Don't even bother begging for your life because it's not happening. From the first time I laid eyes on you, I knew you were a snake in a suit, but I didn't take you as an idiot to try to pull something like this. I couldn't care less, but I would like to give my father a reason so why? Why did you set him up?"

He sat all the way up. "Look, please don't kill me. I have a daughter–"

I tuned him out as I reached and grabbed a pillow. I placed it over the gun and repeated the question. "Fuck your daughter and all that shit you're talking. Again, why did you try to set him up?"

"It was all business. I signed a deal to set your father up. In return, they promised to let me walk away free. It was a win-win situation. I could take over your father's region and stay out of jail. You have to understand, it was just business."

I laughed. "You really think they were going to allow you back on the streets and let you fly under the radar? As soon as they had Dom under the jail, they would've came for you again."

He looked at me with shock.

"Didn't think about that, did you? I know. I understand though, Odney. This was all business."

A hopeful smile came across his dry, thin lips. "Just business. Exactly. So, we can forget about this and–"

"Forget about what?" I doubled over in laughter. "Nah, my nigga, you can't walk out of here but since I'm pressed for time, I won't torture you and feed you to my dogs like I want to." I aimed the pillow at his head. "Consider this business."

Pop! The gun shot, muffled by the pillow, met its desired target in the middle of his head. His eyes were still wide open as he sat upright.

"All right, let's go my nigga," Melo said from behind me.

I took one last look at him before I left, making my way out the same way I came. Once out front, I saw Derria in the driver's seat cruising slowly in front of the house I just came out of. My heart skipped a beat and I panicked. What the fuck was she doing? I looked up and down the street before jumping in the passenger seat and letting the seat all the way back.

"Drive!" I yelled.

She jumped from the bass in my voice and drove off.

"Can't you drive faster than that? Drive this muthafucka!" I yelled.

"I can't when you keep yelling at me!" she screamed with tears running down her eyes.

I instructed her to pull over so we could switch seats. I felt bad for yelling at her. I knew I shouldn't have brought her green ass along with me, but I felt like I had no choice. I had given her specific instructions to not get out the car and she had moved the muthafucka!

She sniffled and wiped her tears.

"Look, Ri-Ri. I'm sorry for yelling at you but I just did some real foul shit. I told you to not move for a reason. I didn't want shit to happen to either of us. I know you're not used to this street shit but just listen to me from now on."

She nodded her head. "I'm sorry, Zae. The house we were parked in front of called the police because they thought I was stealing their damn mail."

"Wait, cops was in the neighborhood?"

"Just one car."

"What did he say? Was he looking around? Did you get a ticket?" I asked her.

"No, he told me to move the car, gave me a warning, and left."

I let out a sigh of relief. She had a nigga scared for a minute.

"But he did take down my tag number for some reason."

TILT MY CROWN TO THE STREETS
Johnazia Gray & Danielle Offett

As long as he didn't see me go in and leave the house, we were good and in the clear. "Again, I'm sorry for yelling at you. I'm gonna drop you off at the rehab spot and you're gonna forget about it. Don't talk to anyone about it, do you understand?"

She nodded her head. This was our little secret.

CHAPTER NINETEEN
DOLA

Early in the mornings when I think about you

Yeah - I hit you like "what you sayin'?"

In the mornings when I wanna fuck you

Yeah - I hit you like "what you sayin'?"

As Jeremiah blared through the speakers, I slowly stripped in front of Chazae. His eyes were low from the mixture of weed and liquor we'd indulged in, but I could still feel them sexually assaulting me. Once I slid the last piece of fabric off my body, I made my way toward him on the bed and crawled toward him like a cat. Straddling his naked body, we search each other's eyes to make sure this was what we wanted to do. There would be no turning back.

He grabbed a fistful of my hair and yanked my head back—not too hard but hard enough to let me know he was in control. What he didn't know was that in the bedroom, I was in control. I began to grind on his lap until I felt his penis searching for my opening like it had a mind of its own.

"Damn, bae," he groaned, holding my hips and watching as my wetness coated his stomach and dick. "Stop playing with me and put that shit in."

I ignored him and attacked his neck with a vengeance. I licked and sucked until I heard him whispering my name. He reached to grab me by the pussy but I slapped his hands away before turning around so that my ass was tooted facing him. I arched my back forward the bed and began to bounce my ass on beat with the lyrics.

> *I could fuck you all the time*
> *I could fuck you all the time*

He rubbed his large hand over my ass and massaged them while using the other to play in the pool of wetness he had created. His fingers felt so good inside of me I thought they were made specifically for me. I could only imagine how his dick would feel.

Grabbing both of my legs, he dragged me backwards until my ass was in the air and my kitty was directly in his face. He took a long whiff before I felt his tongue plunge inside of me.

"Ohhhhhh shit!" I yelled.

My words were all the encouragement he needed to go all in. He began to suck and lick on my clit not missing a spot. The music was loud but I could still hear the sounds of him slurping. His tongue could've been part of a circus the way it did tricks on my clit. Each time it flicked across, my body jumped and he led me tighter.

"Don't run now!" he demanded, diving back in head first.

The orgasm building up inside of me couldn't be avoided. I didn't want to cum so quickly but my body didn't agree. I threw my ass back on his face and fucked his tongue. His nails went into my ass cheeks as he flicked his tongue even harder.

"Shittt!" I moaned, letting my juices run into his mouth like a canal.

That orgasm was so breathtaking, I just laid my head on the bed.

Johnazia Gray & Danielle Offett

He slapped me on the ass before flipping me over. "Don't tap out just yet. I been waiting a long time for my pussy. You running from the tongue, don't run from this dick."

He stroked himself while staring down at my body. The lights from the candles flicked softly, landing on his bronze toned body making him look like an Egyptian Warrior. His dick was beautiful. Yes, I said beautiful! It had to be about ten inches and had more than enough girth to fill me up. There was a light ring around the middle of his dick that made me want to lick circles around it.

I grew nervous as he inched it toward me. He must've sensed it because he leaned down and kissed me. The kiss was amazing but it didn't cover the pain I felt below. I screamed and moaned in his mouth as he ripped me open like a born-again virgin.

"Damn, this shit tight!" he moaned, slowly stroking until he found my spot It had been a while since I'd had sex and my toys were nothing compared to this moment. Once my body adjusted to his size and he began to speed up his stroke, a single tear fell from my eyes. He fit me so perfectly.

"Faster," I told him, wrapping my legs around him and forcing him deeper.

Granting my wish, he plunged balls deep and gave me every inch. After a few strokes, he flipped me over and went right back in like he never left.

"Play with that pussy for me," he demanded.

I obliged and used my fingers to do circles around my clit.

"Damn," he moaned, gripping my waist for support.

I was ready to cum but didn't want to leave him hanging again, so I threw my ass back as fast as I could, making sure it jiggled with each thrust.

"Cum with me, daddy!" I called out to him. "Let me know you love this pussy."

"Mmmm! Fuck!" I moaned as another wave of orgasms came back to back.

"Fuck!" he growled. I could feel his dick pulsating inside of me. We held our position for a minute trying to catch our breaths.

"You feel so damn good I don't want to pull out," he admitted, still moving in and out of me.

I felt the same way but couldn't bring myself to speak.

He removed himself and stumbled to the bathroom. I laid out flat on the bed. Seconds later, he returned with a wet rag and wiped me off. Once I was clean, he lay down next to me and passed out.

For this to be our first time, it was magical. I held out long enough and was glad I gave in. If I hadn't had that talk with Mama Shirley and she didn't threaten to beat my ass, I would've never called him back over. Just like Chazae, I was tired as fuck and needed a good rest after that good ass dick. As my eyes began to close, I smiled, glad that it now belonged to me.

*****

"Babe, come on! I don't want to be late to see, Sissy!" I yelled, putting on Princess' jacket.

"Me too! I'm ready to go see Titi! Hurry up, Zazu!" Princess yelled, jumping up and down with excitement.

I swear, to be a man he took just as long as me to get dressed. If he wasn't out all night, he wouldn't have been so damn tired this morning. He told me he was coming over last night at nine and didn't get in until three. I was pissed but too tired to curse him out. Today was a good day for everyone. It was visitation day for Derria and the one and only Dom was getting released. I still didn't know how he was able to pull it off, but I was happy for him and everyone else. After we saw Derria, we were meeting Dom and Charae at his house for a welcome home party.

"I'm ready. Just looking for my phone," he said, lifting up pillows.

Princess snickered and removed his phone from her pocket. "I wanted to play games on it in the car, Zazu."

He shook his head and picked her up. "Aight, Lady P, you can play on it. Just let me know if somebody calls."

"What if it's one of your old lady friends like last time?" Princess asked innocently.

I shot daggers at him ready to go the fuck in.

"What do you say when a guy calls?" he asked her.

"Hold on a second."

"And what do you say when a lady calls?" he quizzed.

"You got the wrong number tramp!"

Everyone laughed and headed to the car.

"I don't know about that tramp part but you got it right," I told her. "Come on, *Zazu,*" I called him, playfully.

"Chill, woman. Only my favorite girl can call me that. Ain't that right, P?" he asked a smiling Princess.

Once we were in the car, Chazae drove in silence. He always did that when he had a lot on his mind. I rubbed his knuckles.

"What's on your mind?" I asked him.

He didn't even take his eyes off the road. "Tauris."

I already knew what that meant. He was still searching for his ex-best friend and wouldn't rest until he found him. Tauris had betrayed him in the worst way and I understood completely. The real question I wanted to ask was on the tip of my tongue, but I didn't know if I wanted the answer. Even though Lance wasn't my favorite person, he was still the father of my child and I didn't want anything bad to happen to him. I still prayed that he would one day do right by Princess.

"That nigga is dead too," he added.

I looked at Princess who was sleeping peacefully. "Huh?"

"The nigga you're over there thinking about. He's a dead man walking."

I didn't respond. Now it was my turn to look straight ahead. As much as I had prayed about it, I knew once Chazae had his mind set, it was set. Plus, Lance had a part in Semaj being at the trap that day. I knew Chazae wouldn't sleep peacefully until he was buried as well.

The rest of the ride was long and quiet. It took a few hours but once we pulled up, I pushed all thoughts of the bullshit to the back of my mind. I went around and shook Princess a little.

"Come on, baby. Time to go see Titi," I whispered to her.

She looked around and her face lit up. "Yay!!!! Let's go see Titi!"

As soon as her seatbelt was unbuckled, she ran full speed toward the door. I had on heels so luckily, Chazae ran after her.

"Hello, welcome to Recovery Ranch. How may I help you today?" the receptionist asked with a smile.

"We're here to see Derria Stephens."

"Oh yes! She's already waiting on you guys out back on the deck."

We thanked her and went outback.

Johnazia Gray & *Danielle Offett*

"Sissy!" Derria screamed, jumping up to give me a hug. Next, she scooped Princess up in her arms and showered her with kisses. "Titi has missed you so much pretty girl!"

"It's only been a week," Chazae said, leaning in to give her a hug.

"Well, it seems like a month." She pouted, sitting back down in the chair. We all took a seat and just stared at each other. Even though it had only been a week, she looked much better, healthier.

"You look good, Sis. How are you?" I asked her.

She smiled weakly. "I'm doing better. I tried to check myself out the first day I came but somebody," she cut her eyes at Chazae, "paid a police officer an extra ten thousand dollars to bring me back if I tried to leave."

"You damn right!" Chazae said. "And I threatened his life so if he knew what was best for himself, he would make sure you stay put."

She rolled her eyes. "I swear you're like the big brother I never wanted."

He shrugged. "I'll be back. Gotta piss."

As soon as he left, I asked her again. "Are you really okay, Ri-Ri? I mean you look better but are you okay? I know Semaj is still in your heart."

"He will always be in my heart but I'm fine. Not only are they helping me kick my little habit, but I've been seeing a counselor. You know, to help me cope with stuff."

"That's good. I'm happy whenever you're happy," I told her.

"Same here. I see the way you and Chazae are joined at the hip. I was upset at first and felt alone but now, I can honestly say I'm happy you found love."

Johnazia Gray & Danielle Offett

I leaned in and gave her a hug. It meant so much to me that things were finally looking up. She was getting the help and closure she needed, and I was getting the man I needed.

"Derria Stephens?" a voice called, breaking our embrace.

We looked over and saw three uniformed officers.

"Yes?" she asked, standing up and looking from me to them.

"Is there a problem?" I asked, standing next to her and pushing Princess behind me.

"Derria Stephens, you are under arrest for the murder of Odney Romos." He grabbed her arm and cuffed her. "You have the right to remain silent. Anything you say can and will be used against you in a court of law. You have the right to speak to an attorney, and to have an attorney present during any questioning."

What the fuck was going on? I was confused and looked on as Derria cried and screamed my name.

"Mommy, where are they taking Titi!" Princess cried.

"There must be a mistake!" I followed them as they escorted her out of the establishment. "Officer, there must be a mistake! Derria, tell them! This is a fucking mistake!"

Instead of saying anything, she just cried with her head down. No one was listening to me! I spazzed out and began to punch the officer in the back as he walked away from me.

"Let her go! She didn't do shit!" I yelled.

He finally turned around and grabbed my arm. "Ma'am, I'm going to excuse you because of the circumstances. I'm just doing my job. You can have a lawyer contact the precinct with any further questions. I'm sorry," he said and placed Derria in the back of the car.

She didn't even look at me.

Johnazia Gray & *Danielle Offett*

"Who the fuck is Odney Romos?" I screamed. "What is going on?"

As the police cars sped off, I dropped to the ground and screamed. Princess stood next to me, crying as well.

"Babe, what happened? Where's Derria?" Chazae asked, helping me up and pulling me into his chest.

"They took my sister! The police took my fucking sister for the murder of some guy named Odney! I don't even know an Odney!"

He pushed me back a little and looked down at me. "Did they say Odney...Romos?"

I stopped crying and looked up at him. How did he know that?

"What did you do, Chazae?" I asked.

He tried to grab me but I snatched away.

"What did you do?" I pushed him in his chest as hard as I could. "What did you have my sister do?"

"Baby, just calm down. We gotta go. I'll explain in the car," he pleaded, reaching for me.

I walked backwards toward the building with Princess now in my arms. "You stay the fuck away from us! Stay the fuck away!"

The look in his eyes was of defeat and hurt, but it couldn't compete with the pain I was feeling. Everything was finally looking up and now our world was being turned upside down once again all because of Chazae and the street life he chose to live.

To Be Continued…

To reach Danielle Offett for updates on new releases:

Facebook: Danielle Offett

https://www.facebook.com/danielle.offett

Facebook Readers Group (Please Join):

https://www.facebook.com/groups/321223521572444/

Like Page (Please like)

https://www.facebook.com/AuthorDanielleOffett/?ref=aymt_home page_panel

To reach Johnazia Gray for updates on new releases:

Facebook: Johnazia Gray

Facebook Readers Group (Please Join):

https://www.facebook.com/groups/640077029462662/

Like Page: Johnazia Gray Presents (Please Like)

Instagram: Author_Johnazia

Twitter:Author_Johnazia

Want to be notified when the new, hot Urban Fiction and Interracial Romance books are released? Text the keyword "JWP" to 22828 to receive an email notifying you of new releases, giveaways, announcements, and more!

Jessica Watkins Presents is currently accepting submissions for the following genres: African American Romance, Urban Fiction, Women's Fiction, and BWWM Romance. If you are interested in becoming a best selling author and have a complete manuscript, please send the synopsis and the first three chapters to jwp.submissions@gmail.com.

CPSIA information can be obtained
at www.ICGtesting.com
Printed in the USA
LVOW10s1309270318
571320LV00021B/692/P